Her dump

Crow shifter Alice Crawford is living her best life as a salvage artist in Texas. But when her city's namesake, magical stream starts drying up, taking her income with it, she—and everyone else in town—soon find themselves up Shift Creek without a paddle.

When a hot as sin warlock arrives on the scene, Alice thinks he can solve all her problems.

If she can get past his farting familiar.

Warlock Donovan Drake has more secrets than a duck has quacks. His connection to Shift Creek runs deeper than anyone can imagine, and getting turned into a crow the moment he meets Alice is just the beginning of his trouble.

He's falling head over tail feathers for the feisty bird shifter, and if he's not careful, he'll be as exposed as a streaker at the state fair.

Better put your boots on because the shift is getting deep in the Lone Star State!

If you like quirky heroines and smoldering heroes, you'll love this laugh-out-loud paranormal romantic comedy.

CHAPTER ONE

"Holy mother of unnecessarily cruel inventions!" Alice Crawford clenched the steel jaws—which were currently gripping her ankle with a thousand times more force than she could muster—and tried to wrench them apart. "Son of a bitchin' bobcat! That hurts!"

Piercing pain stabbed all the way to the bone, where the trap penetrated skin, and blood trickled down her leg, staining her sock. "Damn it, that was one of two pairs without holes in the toes too."

Gritting her teeth, she clutched the contraption in both hands, trying to pry it open, but the insufferable snare refused to budge. "Evil piece of garbage."

How did a crow shifter find herself in the middle of a farm, entangled in a trap meant to save birds from predators…when she was a friggin' bird herself?

Well, it was shiny, glinting in the moonlight, and she was a crow. How could she resist?

Her mistake had become evident the moment she *swooped* down to grab the culpable object, and it *clamped* down on her leg. The shock had forced her to shift from crow form to human instantly, and thank her lucky stars for that. It would have snapped her bird leg right in half.

Now, she sat with her butt planted firmly in the dirt, her left foot ensnared in the most inhumane of modern torture devices, while the chickens in the coop beside her *bock, bock, bocked* their feathery little heads off, threatening to expose her for trespassing. *Fan-friggin-tastic.*

A pair of eyes gleamed in the moonlight, and a chubby raccoon waddled toward her, chittering like she was laughing her ass off—which she was, knowing Megan. The chickens took one look at her, and pandemonium erupted inside the cage. Their clucking intensified, and they started running around like...well, like chickens with their heads cut off.

"I'm glad I could provide your amusement for the night. Now, help me out of this trap, will you? Those chickens are cackling loud enough to wake the whole town."

The raccoon shifted into human form, and mirth danced in Megan's dark brown eyes as she sidled next to Alice on the ground. "Hi-ho the derry-o, the farmer takes a crow."

"Funny." She clawed at the trap, but the stupid thing must have been broken. It would take the Jaws of Life to pry it apart. Her ankle throbbed, and her foot was going numb. "A little help, please?"

"This is what you get for trying to grab every shiny object you see. Here." Megan pushed the latch on the side of the trap, and the teeth released their hold.

Alice yanked her leg from the device, pressing her hand to the wound to keep the blood from staining her shoe too. "Oh, hello, Pot. My name's Kettle. It's nice to meet you."

"At least I know a trap when I see one." Megan opened the wicked contraption, setting it on the ground before poking the release with a stick. The jaws snapped shut with a *whack*, breaking the stick in two. "You're lucky it only got your leg and not your whole body. How'd you shift so fast?"

Alice shrugged. "I don't know. Instinct, I guess."

"Well, your instinct should tell you to stay away from these." She picked up the device, curling her lip as she examined it.

"That's a raccoon trap, isn't it?"

"Raccoon, fox, stray dog. Anything that might go after his chickens." She glared at the hunk of metal in her hands. "I mean, he has a right to protect his flock, but to make a poor animal suffer?"

The feeling returned to Alice's foot, and she sucked in a sharp breath through her teeth. "I liked it better when it was numb."

"Let's get you to the creek. You'll be good as new in no time." As Megan rose to her feet, the farmhouse porch light flipped on, and the screen door whacked against the façade when a man stormed onto the patio. He squinted, peering into the darkness before cocking his rifle and stomping down the steps.

Alice's pulse thrummed. She couldn't afford another trespassing charge. "See you at the creek."

"Not if I see you first." Megan shifted into raccoon form and darted into the brush, dragging the trap behind her.

Scrambling to her good foot, Alice winced against the pain and shifted into crow form. Thankfully, her wings weren't affected, and she took to the sky as the farmer barreled toward the chicken coop.

Her injury made it impossible to tuck her leg beneath her properly, which also made it impossible to fly straight. She tumbled through the air, completing two full barrel rolls before crash landing on the creek bank. With a pained squawk, she righted herself, shaking the pebbles from her feathers before returning to human form once again.

Fresh blood streamed down her leg, and she kicked off her shoe, sliding her sock off her swelling foot. "Mother ducker. That's the last time I help you search for rusty farm equipment. I don't care how much of a commission you're getting on that sculpture, it's not worth this." She gestured at her wound.

"Come on." Megan appeared from the bushes and helped her stand. "Let's get your foot into the water, and then you can berate me for trying to keep our business afloat."

She let Megan absorb most of her weight as she hobbled down to the creek and rested her foot in the shallow stream. The moment the enchanted water washed over her skin, the wound tingled, sparkling magic surrounding the injury as the swelling subsided. Slowly, the gashes from the trap's jaws stitched themselves back together, and within minutes, no trace of the wound remained.

"Ahhh…." The tension in her muscles eased as the pain finally vamoosed. "That's more like it." Alice scooted back onto the bank and slipped on her blood-stained sock and shoe.

Starlight glittered on the surface of the creek, and a cool spring breeze carried the sweet fragrance of wildflowers and honeysuckle.

Megan stared out wistfully over the water. "I

remember when it wouldn't have taken more than two seconds to heal a gash like that. How much longer do you think we have?"

"I don't know." Rising to her feet, Alice draped an arm around her best friend's shoulders and gazed at the creek. Once vast and wide, the shallow stream now meandered along the narrow, rocky path, no more than two inches deep in some places. This section of the creek, nearest the bubbling springs from which it originated, would reach her waist if she waded into the center. Fifteen years ago, no one could touch bottom.

She wiggled her foot. What would they do when the creek dried up? How would the town survive? "The full moon is next week."

Megan sighed. "It hasn't reversed flow in the past six months. Can we even call ourselves Shift Creek anymore?"

"It is the official name of the town, and it had that name before the creek got its magic." Once nothing more than forest and farmland nestled in the Texas Hill Country, the town was founded by a motley crew of shifters. No, not the band. A sleuth of bears, a gaze of raccoons, a clutter of bobcats, and a murder of crows all joined together to live in harmony in Shift Creek.

Back in the 1800s, a powerful warlock blessed the creek, giving it healing powers for supernatural beings. Every full moon, the stream reversed flow, rejuvenating the magic and creating a great marketing gimmick for drawing tourists to the town.

The springs that sourced the creek filled it with tons of minerals and junk that the mundies—AKA humans— thought were good for them, so the townsfolk capitalized on it, creating a spa that catered to both the supes and mundies. The water didn't do much more for the mundane than any other hot springs would, but for the supes…it was a lifesaver. Literally.

The town prospered for almost two hundred years, until the last ancestors of their beloved warlock moved away, taking their magic with them. Apparently, the blessing spell was contingent on someone from the Rainecourt bloodline living in the town because, when Marcus Rainecourt packed up his kids and skedaddled to New York thirty-something years ago, that was when the trouble started.

Well, not on the exact day. It took several years for the townsfolk to realize there was a problem. With the drought that hit the Hill Country and the construction of a highway a few miles away, the lowering water level seemed like it was due to natural—or mundy—causes in the beginning. They didn't realize the magical source of the problem until the torrential rains that flooded the area did nothing to restore their namesake creek. And the slew of witches and warlocks they'd called in to revive the spell hadn't been able to do a damn thing to fix it.

"Has the supe committee had any luck contacting the warlock?" Megan asked.

"Didn't I tell you? Mr. hoity-toity Marcus, who thought he was too rich and fancy for our town, ticked off the wrong sleuth of bear shifters. Last month, they found him mauled outside his cabin upstate. Something about a spell he gave them going wrong." Alice leaned her back against a tree trunk and crossed her arms. "We're looking for his sons now, but they're MIA."

And if they were anything like their father, even if the committee could contact them, they'd refuse to help.

"How do people from a family that rich and powerful go MIA?" Megan put her hands on her hips. "You'd think they'd have people. Even their people probably have people."

"Oh, we've spoken to their people. Matthias refuses to return our calls, and Griffin is apparently off the grid in a jungle somewhere." She chewed her bottom lip and stared at the water.

Alice joined the supe committee two months ago, when the mundies of the town formed their own group to come up with a solution. She joined both groups, actually, acting as a mundy to spy on those who believed the supernatural origin of the creek was merely legend.

"If you do wrangle one of them, and they come here, be sure to let me know." Megan grinned devilishly. "I'll be a one-woman welcome committee, if you catch my drift."

Alice rolled her eyes. "You're going to catch *something* one of these days."

"Don't be jelly of my social life, babe. You'll always be my BFF."

"Trust me, I'm not jelly." Alice laughed. "Which one do you want to welcome?"

"Either. You know they're both gorgeous."

"How would I know that?"

Megan's mouth fell open. "Don't tell me you've never seen a picture. They're supernatural celebrities, so they're all over the internet. They're so rich, even the mundies know who they are, though they think they're a family of venture capitalists." She tugged her phone from her pocket and typed on the screen.

Alice shook her head. "One: people shouldn't be called celebrities just because they're rich. That term should be reserved for people with talent."

"I'm happy to audition either one of them. Look." Megan shoved the phone in her face.

Alice took it from her, waving it in the air as she spoke. "And two: Even if they were real celebrities, I still wouldn't be following their lives. I love the art, not the artist."

"But look." Megan stilled her hand, and Alice finally took notice of the screen. "That's Matthias. Doesn't he have a powerful, *don't eff with me* look about him? Very alpha."

With dark brown hair and icy blue eyes, Matthias Rainecourt looked like a man not to be trifled with. "He probably likes his women dumb and silent. Next."

"Maybe." Megan eyed the image. "He does have a coldness about him, doesn't he? Still hot though." She swiped the screen. "Griffin is my favorite of the brothers. He's ruggedly handsome, don't you think? And he's always off helping people in third-world countries, so I'd have plenty of time to miss him."

Griffin had a warmer expression. With softer lips and eyes a slightly darker shade of blue, he looked like he might possess at least an ounce of kindness. Alice made a mental note to focus her search on Griffin. He'd be the one most likely to help them. *If* they could track him down.

She handed Megan the phone. "Except, when he disappears, he's really gone. We've been trying to contact him for a month."

"He'll come back. They always do." Megan dropped to her knees to rummage through the bushes. "Ah. Here it is." She pulled out the trap that had ensnared Alice on the farm. "This will make the perfect set of teeth for my bear sculpture."

Alice fisted her hands on her hips. "We're not thieves...anymore."

"My raccoon would beg to differ."

"You have to return that. We're *salvage* artists, remember? We make art from discarded things…not stolen things."

Megan held the trap to her chest. "He left it outside on the ground. Technically…"

"It's a trap, Meg. It's supposed to be outside on the ground. What are you gonna do when Farmer Tucker walks by the shop and sees his stolen trap in a piece of art? What do you think *he's* gonna do?"

She shrugged, pouting her lower lip. "Admire my talent and commission his own piece."

Alice threw her arms in the air, letting them drop at her sides. "He's going to call the cops."

Megan huffed. "Fine. I'll take it back. These things should be illegal, though."

"Write a letter to your congressman."

"Maybe I will."

"Good. I'm gonna call it a night. See you at the shop tomorrow?"

"I'll be there with bells on."

"Please. No bells. Just be there." A few months ago, Alice jokingly said she needed to put a bell on her friend when Megan startled her for the umpteenth time. Meg took it literally and wore a string of the noisy suckers around her neck for a week, jingling all over the place and giving Alice a headache.

"You got it." Megan's body shimmered, a mist of pale pink sparkles dancing around her form as she shifted into her raccoon. She chittered a goodbye and scurried toward the farm, dragging the trap behind her.

With tourism at an all-time low, they were hurting for

cash as it was. They couldn't afford another arrest, especially a theft charge.

Alice sighed, taking one last look at the waning creek before calling on her crow. Her body shimmered in green, her magical signature color—which happened to match her eyes. How cool was that? And she morphed from a five-foot-eight brunette into a one-foot-seven black crow.

With a flap of her wings, she took to the sky, soaring above the trees toward town when a light shining in the corner of her eye caught her attention. Was that coming from Rainecourt Manor?

Her little heart fluttered in her chest as she altered course and headed west toward the abandoned house. Someone on the committee must have gotten through to the brothers. *Halleluiah*, the town was saved!

She flapped harder, elation fizzing in her veins as the mansion came into view. From the outside, you'd never know the place had sat empty for the past thirty-something years. A groundskeeper, who lived in a one-bedroom cottage on the property, kept the place immaculate. The lawn was always mowed, and the paint had never peeled.

Inside, who knew? She imagined lots of chandeliers and expensive furniture covered in sheets, a thick film of dust layered on everything, the stagnant air smelling of mildew like an old haunted house.

Or, heck, they were rich. If they could afford to pay a groundskeeper all these years, maybe they ran the AC and kept it a comfortable seventy-four degrees inside at all times.

One thing was for certain, though. Never in all the time Alice had flown around the place had she seen a light on inside.

She swooped toward the balcony, landing on the

railing and ruffling her feathers before hopping closer to the window. Inside, she glimpsed a stack of boxes and a four-poster dark wood bed with a deep-burgundy duvet. A matching chest of drawers sat against the opposite wall, and…was that a fainting couch? Alice blew a puff of breath through her nostrils. Based on what she'd learned about Marcus Rainecourt, his wife probably used it regularly.

A shadow moved in the corner, and her heart rate kicked up again. If she had fingers, she would have crossed them that the person it belonged to would be Griffin. Truth be told, she didn't know much about either brother. She didn't keep up with the tabloids, and they were both little when their father dragged them to New York, so none of the townsfolk had much intel on them either.

Their father, Marcus, was remembered as a hard-ass warlock who looked down his nose at everyone, including the other witches and warlocks in town. He considered the residents of Shift Creek simpletons—never mind the fact he was born and raised here too. Rumor had it he sold spells on the black market to make his millions. Alice would rather be a simpleton than a criminal.

Hey, trespassing didn't count. If she'd stayed in crow form while digging through the junkyard, she never would have gotten caught. Sometimes a girl needed to use her hands. *Don't judge.*

The balcony door stood open, probably to air the place out. Even if they had run the AC for the past thirty-something years, the inside must've smelled dusty. Alice hopped along the railing, getting as close as she dared, when a masculine grunt emanated from inside.

"Where is it, Martin?" His voice was deep and a little bit rumbly. It was also kinda velvety at the same time, like rocky road ice cream—how the smooth chocolate melted in your mouth, and then you hit a nut or a marshmallow, and those little bumps were what gave it flair.

"How should I know? You packed the boxes." The responding voice held a higher, nasally pitch that didn't sound quite human.

"It wasn't in a box. It was in the satchel with you." Despite being obviously perturbed, something about the man's voice made Alice shiver in a good way. *Mmm...* She had a sudden craving for ice cream.

As she leaned toward the open door, the man came into view. He was tall and slightly tanned, with broad shoulders and muscular legs. His dress slacks and blue button-up had obviously been tailored to fit him perfectly, and as he bent over to peer inside one of the boxes, those fabulously tailored slacks conformed to his backside like they'd been painted on. *Yum.*

He straightened and turned, revealing a strong jawline and sharp cheekbones. His face might have been harsh if not for his full lips—which were currently turned down in a frown—softening his features. Instead, the total package made for one fine specimen of a man. *Sweet sugar*, he was beautiful.

This man had an air of authority, of power, like a Rainecourt, but he looked nothing like the pictures she'd seen of Matthias and Griffin. Rather than piercing blue, his eyes were dark brown. Mysterious. Even in his current mood, they held a look of kindness the brothers lacked. And his hair was light brown...or would it be called dirty blond? Either way, unless he'd dyed it, his locks didn't match the dark mahogany of the Rainecourts in the photos.

Her heart sank. If he wasn't a Rainecourt, he couldn't

save the creek. So what was he doing here? She didn't recall seeing a for sale sign on the property.

Oh well. She'd focus on tracking down Griffin this week. With any luck, she'd have a lead by the next committee meeting.

"I don't remember seeing it in the satchel." The nasally voice had come from a furry little critter who currently sat atop one of the large boxes. About a foot and a half long from nose to tail, the mongoose had brown fur and beady eyes. Yep, it was a talking mongoose.

A familiar. *So at least he is a warlock! Maybe he knows the Rainecourts.*

Shifters, like Alice and Megan, were limited to the abilities of their animal when they took on their form— aside from their minds, of course. They kept their human intelligence, but they lacked the vocal cords needed to actually speak.

Familiars, on the other hand, were magical critters who acted as helpers for the lucky witches and warlocks who were able to catch them. They were rare, and until tamed, they lived in the forest with their non-magical cousins. Only super-powerful beings could tell them apart from mundane animals and catch them, which said a lot about Mr. Hottie in there. Oh, and because they were magical creatures who didn't shift, familiars could talk in animal form.

Must be nice. But they had no human form, and their intelligence never surpassed that of a ten-year-old, so the vocal cords were the only thing Alice envied. That and the way Mr. Hottie picked up this familiar, cradling him against his chest and stroking his fur.

I've got something you can stroke. She cawed at her own joke.

The mongoose snapped his head toward her. "Dinner!" He scrambled over the warlock's shoulder and leaped to the floor, scurrying toward the balcony door.

Surely, he didn't mean *she* was dinner. Did he?

He stopped beneath her, sitting up on his hind legs and pressing his little paws together. "Here, birdie, birdie."

Holy crap. He did want to eat her!

He leaped toward her, swiping his claws like he, an animal, actually thought he could have a shifter for dinner. In his defense, he probably didn't realize what she was, but still…

Alice screeched and flapped her wings, taking to the air and dropping a little present on his head before flying around to the front yard.

"Ah! She shit on me!" the familiar whined as she flew away.

Okay, maybe it wasn't the most ladylike thing to do, but she was in bird form. *If it looks like a crow and sounds like a crow…* Not her finest moment, true, but the damn thing wanted to eat her.

She soared over the silver Audi parked in the horseshoe driveway. The metallic paint glinted in the moonlight, so she circled above it, taking in the view. Hey, she was a crow. She liked shiny things.

As she started to fly away, something near the road caught her eye. Dark silver with a soft green glow, it sat atop a trash bag inside a garbage can, so it was fair game, right? *Totally fair game.*

She swooped down and snatched it, taking to the air again and flying home.

CHAPTER TWO

Alice shoved the last bite of ice cream cone into her mouth and wiped her hands on her skirt. Meg would strangle her if she knew she stopped by Milly Moo's and didn't bring her anything, so it was best to get rid of the evidence before returning to the gallery.

The sun shone high in the midday sky, warming her skin while the crisp breeze worked to cool her down again. Spring—all three weeks of it—was beautiful in the Texas Hill Country. Bluebonnets and buttercups blanketed the ground, adding a splash of color to the deep green palette, and being outside for longer than half an hour was more than bearable... It was downright pleasant. It wouldn't be long before the heat became sweltering, though, so Alice enjoyed the walk from city hall to the ice cream shop and finally back to the gallery.

Shifted Treasures was situated along the main town square, sandwiched between a clothing boutique and a bakery. Megan's junkyard sculptures occupied one display window, while Alice's wall art, made from reclaimed wood and discarded metal, was showcased in the other. An open sign hung in the window of the red wooden door, though it would be permanently switched to closed if they couldn't fix the creek's magic soon.

She checked her fingers for signs of chocolate—that rocky road really hit the spot—before opening the door and striding inside.

"And? What did you find out about the mystery man?" Megan didn't look up from her spot behind the counter as she soldered a wing made from fork tines onto a soup can flamingo. She'd swept her brown hair into a high ponytail, and a bulky pair of safety glasses sat perched on her nose.

"He's not a Rainecourt." Alice stuffed her purse onto a shelf beneath the counter, and Megan gripped her shoulder.

"You sneaky little weasel. I can't believe you went to Milly Moo's and didn't bring me anything."

Busted. Alice tugged from her grasp, straightening. "It would have melted on the way."

"I don't mind melty ice cream."

"I'm sorry. I paid the rent, and I…" She couldn't afford the treat for herself, really, but after last night, the thoughts of rocky road refused to leave her mind.

Megan slid the glasses to the end of her nose and peered over them, crossing her arms. "I would have given you money."

"I didn't know I was going. It was a last-minute decision. Can you ever forgive me?"

She pursed her lips, screwing her mouth to the side before laughing. "I'm just giving you a hard time. I had a massive blueberry muffin on my way in this morning, and I didn't bring you one. We're even."

Alice grinned. "I guess we are. How did you know I had ice cream?"

"I can smell it on you." She tugged her hair from the band, letting it cascade around her shoulders. "And you've got a little on the corner of your lip."

Alice wiped her mouth with the back of her hand. "Gone?"

Megan nodded. "So, Mr. Hottie didn't turn out to be a Rainecourt. That's a shame. Who is he?" She dropped the plastic glasses on the counter and wiped her hands on a towel.

"His name is Donovan Drake, and that's all anyone at city hall knows about him." *Donovan Drake.* His name tasted sweet on her tongue...or maybe it was the remnants of the ice cream. Either way, it was a nice name. Masculine. Sexy even.

"I guess the house wasn't on the market long, then? I can't imagine why anyone who can afford a place like that would want to move to a small town like this."

"Now you sound like a Rainecourt." Alice crossed her arms. "There's nothing wrong with this town, and the house was never officially on the market. Mr. Hottie showed up with the deed yesterday morning and moved in. Probably traded his soul for it based on the previous owner."

"Now, now. The black-market spells thing is nothing more than a rumor." Megan stepped around the counter. "Let's not judge my future ex-husband's dead father too harshly."

Alice scoffed. "Not judge? Not only did Marcus have a holier-than-thou attitude, but he up and left the town to die."

"True."

"And we get judged constantly. 'Ew, you're a crow. Do you eat carrion?' Or 'It's not art if it's made out of junk.' Or my personal favorite, 'You're thirty. When are you going to find a husband?'"

Megan groaned. "I hate that one. Have they seen the selection of men in this town?"

"What selection?"

"Exactly!" Megan laughed. "Come in the back. I want to show you the bear sculpture."

"You finished it?" Alice followed her through a blue beaded curtain into their workroom.

"Ta-daaa…" Megan gestured to the five-foot-tall sculpture.

Made out of a muffler, rebar, oil cans, and various other metallic objects, the bear rendering stood on its hind legs, lifting its paws, its mouth open to reveal massive teeth made from… Wait a minute…

"You said you were going to return the trap to the farm." Alice lifted a brow accusingly. "We don't make art from stolen goods."

"I did return it." She traced a finger along the metal teeth. "I disassembled it before leaving it by the chicken coop, but all the parts were there. I can't help it if Farmer Tucker is too bird-brained to put it back together."

"Watch it, trash panda. There's nothing diminutive about a bird's brain."

Megan lifted her hands. "Sorry. Anyway, he threw it out, which made it fair game. Just like your new necklace."

Alice gripped the pendant she'd plucked from Mr. Hottie's trash can last night. "Well, if you promise he'd discarded it…" Who was she to judge?

The amulet consisted of a two-inch cylindrical green crystal. One end was nestled inside a beat-up, dark gray metal hood, which hung from a long, tarnished chain, and the other end had a chunk missing from the stone as if it had been carelessly dropped on the concrete.

She'd cleaned it up, attempting to polish the metal, but whatever it was made of, it refused to shine. The wealthy Mr. Drake probably thought it clashed with his pristine aesthetic, so he tossed it. Alice, on the other hand, found beauty in imperfection, and this clunky piece of jewelry called to her.

The tinkling of bells signaled a customer had entered, and Megan turned to her. "What do we sell?"

"Functional, quirky home aesthetics and gifts." Because actually calling their art *art* either made people scoff or feel like they couldn't appreciate it. "Let's sell some A-R-T."

Donovan Drake settled into a wrought-iron chair on the coffee shop sidewalk. After setting his iced latté on the table, he situated his tan leather satchel on the chair next to him and gazed out into the square.

Shift Creek was a quaint town, charming with its little shops and their cheerfully painted storefronts. An old-timey general store occupied the space next to the coffee shop, and an eclectic art gallery stood across the square. He'd passed an elementary school on his way into town with a well-kept wooden playground surrounded by a fence. It was the perfect place to raise a functional family. *Functional* being the keyword there.

He could understand why his father had chosen to move. To be taken seriously in black-market magic, warlocks had to make a name for themselves in large cities.

But why the man had kept this place secret from Donovan and his brothers, he wasn't sure. A magical creek ran through the town. A creek with supernatural healing properties…a possible way to fix his broken magic…yet his father never spoke of it. It was like the man didn't want Donovan to be a warlock.

He didn't, you bastard. He didn't even want you. His jaw clenched at the thought. His father was dead now, so it didn't matter what Marcus Rainecourt wanted.

As he unlocked the satchel and folded back the flap, a cloud of funk that smelled like a cross between hard-boiled eggs and microwaved broccoli assaulted his senses. He leaned back, wrinkling his nose and fanning the air as his familiar poked his head from the bag.

"For Christ's sake, Martin, are you trying to kill yourself? Next time, wait until you have some ventilation before you let one rip." Donovan had just given the mongoose a bath last night, after a crow took revenge on him for his attack. Now his fur would smell like fart for at least the next six hours.

"What?" The mongoose lifted his nose, sniffing the air. "I don't smell anything."

Donovan shook his head and pulled a journal from the satchel, fanning it to the side to remove the stench before setting it on the table. "Maybe another trip to the vet is in order? This much gas can't be normal."

"You're joking, right?" Marty climbed onto the table, sitting upright and wiping his face with his paws. "Last time I went to the vet, they poked a plastic stick up my ass for no reason."

"They were checking you for worms, Martin." He opened the journal and unfolded a yellowing sheet of paper, gazing at the script handwriting. A family tree dating back to the early eighteen-hundreds cascaded down the page. It was left to him along with the deed to the manor here. Why, he had no clue.

"I don't have worms." Marty inched toward him, resting his paws on the journal. "And you only call me Martin when you're in a mood. Why are you in a mood?"

Donovan tugged the book toward himself and folded the paper, tucking it between the pages. "I don't know. Maybe it's because we've lost the one magical item that could have solved all my problems." He slammed the book shut and pressed his fingers to his temples. "You're sure you don't remember seeing it?"

"I don't, boss. I'd tell you if I did. You musta left it in New York."

"I specifically remember putting the amulet in the satchel with you. It was in this pocket." He dipped his hand into the front of the bag, rummaging around as if he might actually find the artifact.

He'd dumped the entire contents, turning the satchel inside-out, when he arrived at the manor. Before that, he'd unpacked two boxes of rare and expensive artifacts—things he didn't dare leave behind in New York—tossing the paper and bubble wrap out for the garbage collectors to pick up this morning. Perhaps he'd accidentally tossed the amulet too.

No, he would never be so careless.

"I'm sorry, boss. We'll figure something else out. We always do. You and me are a great team."

He grabbed his iced coffee and took a sip. Cold and refreshing, the milk tamed the bitter espresso, much like Marty was trying to do to him now. But Donovan's bitterness ran bone-deep.

A bastard child resulting from his father's escapade

with a prostitute, Donovan was only accepted in the Rainecourt home after a DNA test proved his heritage. His mother had left him on the doorstep as an infant, and he was lucky a housekeeper had found him and not the master warlock himself.

She'd listed Marcus Rainecourt as the father on the birth certificate, but the old man changed Donovan's last name to Drake, after his mother, to prove he had no interest in raising him as his own.

When Donovan failed to develop magic as he matured, his father blamed his mother's human blood, though Matthias and Griffin's mother was human as well. Donovan seemed mundane, but his aura naturally held a faint, colorless glow, which indicated his magical lineage.

Pushing up his sleeve, he fingered the bracelet on his wrist. An enchanted silver coin with a hole through the middle was attached to a brown leather strap. The magical artifact cloaked his pathetic aura, creating the illusion he possessed the same level of power his family name suggested.

He *should* have had powers, and this place was the answer to his prayers. He could feel it in his bitter bones.

Donovan had done everything imaginable to activate his magic, but to no avail. After enduring his father's inhumane attempts throughout his childhood, as an adult, he'd gone to healers and scoured the dark web for artifacts to release his powers. Finally, he'd visited a seer last year, who gave him a prophecy.

The old woman had said he did indeed have magic locked inside him. That part he understood. The rest was cryptic, as prophecies are, and made no sense until he received the deed to the manor here and learned about the magical creek.

She'd said the source of his power flowed through his destiny and only by sacrificing the magic of another would he break the ties that bound him.

He'd thought that was the end of his prophecy, but as he'd stood to leave, the woman had clutched his wrist and informed him of an impending deadline. If Donovan didn't unlock his magic by his thirty-fifth birthday, his powers would be gone for good.

He would turn thirty-five next month.

Marty put his paws on Donovan's hand. "If the creek really does heal magical beings, you won't need the amulet anyway."

"I don't have an illness. My powers are locked, and I need the magic of another to unlock them. The amulet would have let me take the magic from the creek and use it to free my own."

"You don't know that for sure. You never got it to work before."

He narrowed his eyes at the familiar. "I'm aware of my inabilities."

It was true he hadn't been able to make the amulet work, but that didn't mean it wouldn't. Donovan dealt in magical artifacts. Buying and selling was how he earned his living. Most of the time, an artifact's magic could be wielded by anyone—even the mundane. His father's black-market business gave him access to all sorts of sellers, and part of Donovan's job was to acquire artifacts that had fallen into human hands, returning them to the magical community where they belonged.

The mundane couldn't behave themselves with computers on social media, much less with an artifact that granted magical abilities. Most of the time, humans couldn't figure out how they worked, but when they did...

The supernatural world was kept secret for a reason, and his business helped keep it that way.

The only magic Donovan had ever wielded himself came from one of the many artifacts he bought and sold, and the amulet promised to allow him to siphon the magic from another, keeping it for himself. Of course, he'd never steal another living being's magic. That would be something his father would do. But a self-restorative body of water could do without its power until the next full moon, when it could heal itself by reversing flow.

Now, with the amulet MIA, he'd have to hope the creek really was as powerful as the website touted. Otherwise, he'd come all this way for nothing.

No, not nothing. He was the new owner of a vast, pristine piece of property. At the very least, he could put the place up for sale while he was here.

"Human alert. Three o'clock." Marty dropped to all fours and squeaked like a mundane mongoose as two women approached.

"How cute," the brunette said. "Can I pet your ferret?"

Marty growled low in his throat, and for a moment, Donovan considered telling her yes to get even with the mongoose for farting inside his satchel. His familiar wasn't fond of being petted by anyone other than him, but in his current mood, Donovan didn't want to deal with the whining that would follow.

"Better not. He needs to see the vet soon."

As if to drive the point home, Marty let another stink bomb rip before scurrying into the satchel to hide. One woman covered her nose, while the other curled her lip in disgust and dragged her away.

Donovan laughed as the women crossed the street, and he sipped his latté, gazing at the art shop across the way.

"Shifted Treasures. Functional, quirky home aesthetics and gifts." He rose to his feet, shielding his eyes from the sun. Sculptures and wall art occupied the display windows. Salvage art. If anyone knew where to find junk that had gone missing, it would be the artist inside.

CHAPTER THREE

Alice padded behind Megan into the storefront, and her shoulders slumped when she found her mom standing by the counter with two Styrofoam cups in her hands. "Hey, Mom."

"Don't sound so glum, little chick. I brought you ladies some of our famous sweet tea." She smiled, deepening her laugh lines. Other than that, Alice's mom hardly had any wrinkles to speak of. With her deep-green eyes and black hair, Alice was a mirror image of her mother…if the mirror subtracted ten years. Seriously, her mom was twenty-five years older than her, but they could pass for sisters.

Being called her "mini-me" used to ruffle Alice's feathers, but if she could age as gracefully as her mother, she was glad of it now. *Don't look a gift horse—or great genes—in the mouth.*

"Thank you, Janice." Megan elbowed Alice on her way to take the drinks. "That was so nice of you. How are things going at The Crow's Nest?"

Alice's parents, Janice and Edward, ran the town's most

popular—and only—café in the square. Of course, all the supes understood the name for what it was. They lived above the restaurant, so it was literally their nest. But for the humans passing through, the nautical theme implied the place was named after the lookout point attached to the highest mast of a ship.

"Slower than it should be, but rumor has it that's about the change." Her eyes brimmed with excitement. "I heard one of the Rainecourt brothers is back."

Alice pressed the straw to her lips and sucked in a giant gulp of her drink. It was overly sweet, but that was how Texans liked their tea. "I hate to be the one to pluck your tailfeathers, but the man who moved into the manor isn't a Rainecourt."

Her mom fisted her hands on her hips. "Are you sure? Patricia is the only real estate agent in town, and she said the house was never for sale."

"I'm sure. I just got back from city hall."

"Oh." Her posture deflated as she slipped her purse strap on her shoulder. "I'm going to have words with Patricia. She ruffled my feathers for nothing. And here I thought I was bringing good news."

"Sorry, Mom. Thanks for the tea, though." Alice walked her to the door. "Tell Dad not to work too hard."

She laughed. "He hardly works."

Alice waved as her mom crossed the street, and then she leaned her head back inside the studio. "I'm going to prop the door open. It's nice outside."

"Good idea." Megan returned to soldering her bird statue, and Alice grabbed the concrete-filled bucket, which looked like a flowerpot with a metallic daisy growing from it, and positioned it in front of the open door.

As she bent over to slide it into place, her new amulet

swung forward, catching the sunlight like a prism, scattering it onto the ground in a sparkling green-tinted rainbow. She straightened, and her eyes locked on Donovan Drake. He stood across the street, shielding his eyes from the sun as he looked right at her.

Her breath caught, and she walked backward into the store, tripping over the doormat and nearly falling on her butt. Luckily, she caught herself on a multi-media mermaid statue before she could eat tile, but as she jerked on the plastic faux-seashell top to straighten herself, the statue's left boob came off in her hand. "Sorry. I'll fix that." She couldn't let the poor fish-girl go around lopsided.

"What's got you so spooked?" Megan scurried around and took the taillight-turned-teat, setting it on the counter.

Alice swallowed hard before daring to peer out the open door. "Holy mermaid mammaries. He's coming this way."

"Who?" Megan sidled next to her, cocking her head. "Well, hello, handsome. Is he who you're scared of?"

"That's Donovan Drake." Alice gripped the amulet, dropping it down the neck of her shirt as she stepped to the side, out of view. "Why is he coming here?"

"To buy some art, of course. He looks like a man who could appreciate what we do." Megan tapped a finger to her lips. "The more pertinent question is: Why is he carrying a purse?"

Alice dared another glance. "It's not a purse. It's a satchel. He has to have somewhere to put his mongoose in public."

"Most men keep them in their pants."

Alice grabbed her arm, dragging her away from the

door. "I'm talking about his familiar. What are you talking about?"

She grinned. "His dick, of course."

"You're impossible."

"For him, I'd be easy. You didn't call dibs, did you? Otherwise, I might get *really* familiar with him."

"I did see him first." Alice bit her bottom lip and leaned so she could see out the window. Donovan paused to let a woman pushing a baby stroller pass before continuing his trek in her direction. Her stomach fluttered. He was even more attractive in the daylight.

"Okay, you can have him." Megan sounded reluctant, until she winked. "I'm holding out for a Rainecourt, anyway. You better hurry up and find one."

"I'm working on it." She straightened her spine as Donovan paused in the doorway, wiping his shoes on the welcome mat before adjusting his satchel and stepping through the threshold.

He wore a dark blue blazer with matching slacks and a light blue button-up. Like the suit she'd seen him in before, it appeared custom-made, fitting his broad shoulders and muscular thighs perfectly. Every lock of his wavy, light brown hair lay in just the right place, and the set of his dark eyes gave him a mysterious, brooding appearance. *Yum.*

A wad of paper knocked Alice in the back of the head, and she blinked, turning to see where it came from. Megan made a face, gesturing at Donovan. *Crap on a cracker.* How long had she been staring at the man?

She cleared her throat and stepped toward him. "Hi…" The tip of her tongue touched the roof of her mouth as she started to say his name. Luckily, her jaw clamped shut as he made eye contact, her thickening throat not allowing her to commit the faux pas. She sure as heck didn't want to explain why she already knew his name when he'd just arrived in town yesterday.

I watched you unpack from your balcony railing until your mongoose tried to eat me. Then I went to city hall and asked every person in the building until someone told me your name, but I promise I'm not a stalker! Yeah...that would go over really well.

"Hello." He grinned, and the corners of his eyes crinkled. That was good. Crinkles meant he smiled a lot.

"Welcome to Shifted Treasures. I'm Alice. Can I help you find something in particular?" She returned the smile, and his widened, commanding her crow's attention. *Oh, boy.* If her bird had taken notice, she was in a mess of trouble. *That damn mating instinct better not kick in now.*

"Just browsing." He picked up a small aluminum figurine of a frog playing a banjo and chuckled before returning it to the shelf.

"Okay, well, I'm here all day, if you need me." She took two slow steps backward. When he simply nodded, she turned and joined Megan behind the counter.

"Way to sound desperate," Megan whispered out of the side of her mouth.

"How was that desperate? He's a patron in our store, and I offered to help."

"'I'm here all day, if you need me,'" Megan mocked. "You have to *convince* him he needs you, and you do that by playing hard to get. You should have told him you're about to step out. Then he'd know he's running out of time."

"But I'm not about to step out. I just got back."

Megan glared at her, speaking through clenched teeth, "So, step out again."

"You step out."

"Then he'll think he needs *me*."

Alice sighed. "Seriously, Meg. You really are impossible."

"Do you ladies create all this art yourselves?" In the thirty seconds Alice had been bickering with her friend, Donovan had moved to stand directly in front of the counter. Within earshot. *Fan-friggin-tastic.*

Alice scooted to the end of the counter, away from Megan and her badgering. "We do. We also take custom orders if there's something specific you're looking for that you don't see in the store."

"Hm." He nodded and swept his gaze across the room. "It's whimsical. I like it."

"Thank you. I'm full of whimsy, so..." She held in a groan. Full of whimsy? *More like full of crap.*

One corner of his mouth twitched as he gazed at an antique school desk she'd bejeweled with assorted stones and shards of metal. "Where do you find the material?"

Alice squared her shoulders, getting her act together. Yes, he was hotter than asphalt on an August afternoon, but he was still a customer. "Various places. Junkyards, buildings that are being torn down, donations."

"Finding the treasures in people's trash is in our blood," Megan said proudly.

Alice shot her a look. You didn't go around telling polished, sophisticated, downright sexy men that you dug through other people's garbage. Maybe Megan *was* the one who needed to step out before she scared the man away.

"It's all thoroughly cleaned before it's incorporated into a piece. In fact..." Alice padded toward a vintage mirror she'd framed. "This one is made from the reclaimed wood of a historic building in downtown Austin."

"Nice." He peered into the mirror, focusing on her in the reflection.

Donovan Drake had to be the most handsome man she'd ever laid eyes on. She chewed the inside of her cheek, trying to recall a more perfect face, a better body—even through the clothes. Nope, nothing. And something about the way he looked at her made her blood feel all fizzy in her veins.

"So, if someone in this town had lost something... something that most would consider junk, where might they go to find it?"

Alice's stomach sank. It was possible he was talking about the amulet currently hanging inside her shirt. But if she admitted she had it, she'd have to explain what she was doing at the manor in the first place. The home was set so far back from the main road, you'd have to be going there on purpose to even pass by.

But she'd found the necklace in the garbage can, discarded like...well, like trash. And anyway, he was a warlock. Couldn't he cast a locating spell or scry for it if it were that important?

She cleared her throat. "Depending on the size of the lost item, it could be at the junkyard. If it's small, though, it's probably on its way to a landfill. What did you lose?"

He held her gaze, his dark, brooding eyes boring into her, making her pulse race. "Nothing I can't live without. Alice, right? I'm Donovan."

Hot diggity dog. This guy must've had laser vision because he was about to melt her panties off with those mysterious eyes. An amused grin lifted his lips, and it wasn't until she finally dragged her gaze away from his face that she noticed he'd offered his hand to shake.

She slapped her palm against his a little too hard, gripping his hand and shaking it like a madwoman. "Nice to meet you." Releasing her hold, she laced her fingers together as Megan suppressed a giggle.

"The pleasure is mine." Mirth danced in his eyes.

"What brings you to Shift Creek?"

"I heard about your magical stream and had to see it for myself. It really reverses flow on the full moon?"

He'd *heard* about the creek? The man was staying in the ancestral home of the warlock who enchanted it. Surely he knew its condition. "I hate to be the one to tell you this, but it hasn't shifted in six months. It's drying up."

His brow lowered, the look on his face indicating he did *not* know its condition. *Poor guy.*

"I see. That wasn't mentioned on the website." The muscles in his neck tightened as he clenched his teeth.

"It's in the fine print at the bottom. The font is small, and it's red on black, so I can see how you'd miss it." She'd tried to convince the city to make it more prominent on the page—on both the mundy and the supe sites—but when their main source of income was drying up, it wasn't something they wanted to advertise.

He glanced toward the door and lowered his voice. "And the healing properties? Has it lost those too?"

"Not yet. It's slower than it used to be, but it still heals."

"Alice used it to heal her foot last night when she got caught in a farmer's trap," Megan said.

"You were caught in a trap?" Donovan's eyes held concern.

Alice shot Megan a look before shaking her head. "It's a long story. I'm fine."

"Good to hear." He glanced at her feet. "It really healed your wounds?"

She rotated her ankle. "It did."

He nodded, his chest rising and falling as if he'd sighed in relief. The man looked as fit as a brand-new fiddle. What on earth could he need healing for? "I'll just have a look around."

"Great. Let me know if you have any questions." Alice sashayed behind the counter, not even fighting her grin.

"They really need to update that website." Megan unplugged her soldering iron and cleaned up her mess. "The poor man came all this way to watch the creek shift. Well, at least he's got a nice place to stay. I'd love to see the inside of Rainecourt Manor."

"Shh… He doesn't know we know where he's staying." Alice rose onto her toes to get a better view of Donovan as he browsed the artwork. *The man is delicious.*

"He must be so disappointed." She wiggled her eyebrows. "But I'm sure you can make the trip worth his while."

Alice giggled. "One taste of me, and he'd become a permanent resident."

"He seems drawn to the bird sculptures. I'm tempted to tell him he doesn't need aviary art when he can have the real thing right here." Megan elbowed her in jest. "But we really need to make a sale, so I'll keep my mouth shut."

"Mmm… He can have this bird any time he wants it." A burning sensation flashed through Alice's chest, her skin turning to gooseflesh as electricity shot down to her toes. As the feeling dissipated, she shivered and rubbed the back of her neck. "That was weird."

Donovan gasped, and she jerked her gaze toward him in time to see him stiffen before his entire body shuddered. His aura sparkled, the deep-orange turning to green shifter magic, and in an instant, he disappeared behind a display shelf.

"What the heck?" Alice hurried across the floor with Megan on her heels, trying to ignore the aching hole that seemed to be expanding in her chest. A man had collapsed in their store. She'd worry about what just happened to her later.

As she rounded the shelf, the sexy warlock was nowhere in sight. Instead, his satchel lay open on the floor, the mongoose standing with his little back arched, making a mewling sound deep in his throat as he stared at a startled crow.

"Shoo. Nobody eats crow in my presence." Megan moved toward the mongoose, waving her arms, while Alice stood frozen in shock.

The familiar squealed and skittered across the floor, climbing the display shelf and knocking over a picture frame before plowing through a set of handmade wildflower trinkets. Megan snatched a ceramic pot from another shelf, grabbed the mongoose, and shoved him inside before latching the lid closed.

The crow looked at Alice, tilted his head, and then squawked before attempting to take flight. It flapped its wings wildly, gaining air and then crashing into the ground. It continued its path toward the open front door, and Alice's shock finally subsided, turning to panic. She couldn't let that bird get away.

"Stop him!" she shouted, and Megan shoved the doorstopper aside before yanking the door shut.

The crow continued forward, unable to stop, and plowed into the window head-first. He tumbled, smacking his back on the concrete floor and going completely still. *Oh no.*

"Is he a crow shifter too?" Megan set the jar of protesting mongoose on the floor and kneeled beside the bird.

"He's not a shifter." Alice joined her, fisting her trembling hands as her heart pounded. The hollow feeling in her chest expanded, and she knew exactly why. "He's stolen my crow."

CHAPTER FOUR

"What do you mean he's stolen your crow?" Megan shot to her feet and locked the door before grabbing a seat cushion from a chair. "Your crow is part of you. How could he do that?"

"I don't know, but I can feel it's missing, and look..." She scooped the bird into her hands, and Megan set the cushion on the floor. As Alice laid the bird on it, she lifted its wing, revealing a small patch of white feathers on its side. "That's my mark."

"Son of a bitchin' bald eagle." Megan eyed the pot, in which the mongoose chittered away angrily. "How smart do you think his familiar is?"

"I heard them holding a conversation last night." She pulled the pot into her lap and tapped on the lid. "Hey, can you hear me?"

"Of course I can hear you. I'm not deaf." The familiar knocked on the lid.

"I'm going to let you out, but you are not to eat the crow. He's your warlock. Do you understand?"

"Don't eat the crow. Got it. Now let me out before I suffocate."

Alice unlatched the lid, and the mongoose clambered out, skittering in a circle around the bird.

"What's that smell?" Alice wrinkled her nose as a rancid stench rose from the jar.

"Ew." Megan waved a hand in front of her face. "He must have those scent glands like a ferret."

"Or a skunk." She set the jar aside. *Jesus Christ on a unicycle,* the reek was enough to make her gag.

"What did you do to him?" the mongoose demanded. "Is he dead?"

"He did this, not me. And he's breathing...I think." She eyed the bird until the gentle rise and fall of its chest registered in her vision. "Yes, he's breathing."

"Turn him back!"

"I didn't turn him to begin with, so you'd better start talking. How did he do this?"

"You did it!" The familiar raced toward her. His tiny claws dug into her arm as he climbed up to her shoulder. "Where is it?" he squeaked into her ear.

He slid his front paws down her collarbone, ducking his head as he dove into her shirt like a baseball player sliding into home. Alice squealed and jumped to her feet, shaking her blouse and trying to get the damn thing out, but he'd latched onto the underwire in her bra right between her boobs.

"Let go, you little weasel!" She lifted her shirt and grabbed the animal. He released his hold on her girls and instead caught the necklace in his teeth. Wrapping his tiny arms around the pendant, he held on for dear life, refusing to get the heck out of her shirt until Megan yanked on his tail.

"Watch it!" As he spoke, his grip loosened, and Alice jerked him away from her body, dropping him into the jar Megan held toward her.

"That went well." Meg latched the lid, despite the mongoose's squeals of protest, and clutched the jar as he struggled.

Alice stared at the unconscious bird. *Her* bird. How on earth did this happen? And more importantly, how in heaven's name could she get her crow back inside her where it belonged? "When people talk about out-of-body experiences, I never imagined it would be like this."

"Do you think it's possible that you did it?" Megan set the jar on the floor.

Alice couldn't take her eyes off her bird. "How? He's the warlock. I'm just a bottom-feeding shifter."

"Hey, now. We are not bottom feeders. Brains are far more important than brawn, no matter what the wolves and mountain lions try to say."

She crossed her arms. "Well, I obviously didn't do it. I wouldn't have a clue how to even start."

"But why would he take your power? He clearly wasn't prepared for it. His own familiar wanted to eat him, and he had no idea how to fly. Maybe it was your hormones or something. Does anyone in your family have extra powers?"

"No." Megan was right, though. It wouldn't make sense for him to try and steal her magic right there in the store, especially when he had no experience with flying… which was obvious when he'd taken to the air like her drunken Uncle Xavier after an all-nighter at the bar. And Donovan wouldn't have left his bag and his familiar behind. There had to be another explanation.

She gasped. "The amulet." Alice fished the pendant

from her shirt and held it in her hand, lowering her voice so the mongoose wouldn't hear. "Do you think it has powers? I felt a burning sensation in my chest before it happened, right where the amulet was resting against my skin."

"It's possible, but...why would he throw it away? And if it was the amulet's magic, how did you activate it?"

She shook her head, perplexed. "I have no idea."

Megan drummed her nails on the counter. "What were we talking about when it happened? Maybe it was something you said."

Alice let the amulet fall against her shirt. "We were joking about me making his trip to Shift Creek worthwhile."

"That's right. And he was looking at the bird art."

"And I said he could have my bird." She sucked in a sharp breath and lifted the pendant again. "That must be what happened. I *gave* him my crow." Her mouth hung open as she cut her gaze between the amulet, her friend, and her crow.

"So, take it back." Megan gestured to the still unconscious bird.

He must have hit his head pretty hard. *Poor guy's gonna have such a headache.*

"Right. Good idea." Alice stepped toward her crow and gripped the amulet, focusing on taking her other self back. She gritted her teeth, furrowing her brow and tightening her eyes as she attempted to reverse the magic.

"What are you doing?" Megan broke her concentration.

"I'm trying to focus."

"You look like you're trying to poop. Stop it."

Alice glared at her friend. "Fine." She returned her

gaze to the bird. Heavy concentration wasn't working, anyway. Maybe she had to vocalize it. "Give me back my crow."

Green shifter magic glittered around her bird as it morphed into Donovan. The burning returned to Alice's chest, and the electrical sensation buzzed up her limbs, filling the emptiness she'd felt in her core since this whole goddamn ordeal began.

Donovan was still unconscious, but Alice finally felt whole.

"Did it work?" Megan asked.

"I think so. Let me see." She glanced out the window to be sure no mundies were passing by before shifting into her crow form. Flapping her wings, she glided low across the floor, landing on the other side of Megan before shifting back to human. "Thank goodness he took the headache with him."

Donovan groaned, his eyes darting back and forth beneath his lids, and Megan snickered.

"What's so funny?" Alice dropped the necklace back into her shirt.

"You flipped him the bird. Literally." She doubled over with laughter.

Alice tried not to join her, but the shock and absurdity of it all had taken a toll. She chuckled, but when Megan snorted, Alice couldn't help but crack up with her friend. They laughed until tears streamed down their cheeks, and Alice took a deep, shuddering breath.

"If he doesn't wake up soon, we'll have to take him to the creek. He might have a concussion."

"He's almost two-hundred pounds of pure muscle." Megan wiped beneath her eyes. "How would we pull that off without being noticed?"

"It's either that or take him to the hospital, and I don't know how we'd explain what just happened to the mundy doctors. Who knows if human medicine could even help a warlock recover from a spell?"

"True." Megan tapped him on the cheek. "Wake up, sir. We don't want to drag you clear across town to the creek."

"Stop it. Just give him a minute." Alice reached a hand toward him, hesitating before brushing a strand of hair from his face. He responded to her touch, inhaling deeply before his eyelids fluttered.

Fingers gently brushed Donovan's forehead as he came to, the tenderness in the touch making his breath catch. Aside from the witch au pair who raised him, and Griffin's occasional words of encouragement, he wasn't used to being on the receiving end of kindness.

As he turned his head toward the owner of the gentle touch, he knew, without a doubt, it was Alice, the intriguing artist with black hair and emerald eyes. His lids tried to flutter open, but he kept them closed, running the past ten minutes through his mind and trying to understand what had happened.

The moment he'd stepped inside the store, he'd been taken by her beauty, but it was so much more than that. As their eyes met, it felt as if a loose thread in his soul had finally stitched into place, making him almost whole.

He felt a strange connection with the woman, which made no sense at all because he'd never felt a connection to anyone. He never even had a comradery with his own brothers, as they weren't allowed to treat him as family growing up.

When Alice spoke, her voice commanded his attention, calling to something deep inside his soul. He'd stepped away to gather his thoughts, as her mere presence had seemed to short-circuit his brain.

Then he'd stiffened, his body seizing as if an electrical current had run through it, and he'd dropped the floor, sprouting feathers and a beak.

Her aura—and that of her coworker—glittered with nothing more than shifter magic, and he didn't sense the presence of a witch or warlock inside the store. So, who cast the spell that transformed him into a bird?

It was time he opened his eyes and found out.

It took a moment for his blurred vision to focus—the throbbing in his head didn't help—but as his sight cleared, he found the lovely Alice kneeling over him, concern tightening her eyes as she chewed her bottom lip.

"There you are." She smiled softly.

"Thank goodness," her friend said. "We thought we would have to drag your limp body all the way to the creek and roll you in."

Donovan blinked and pushed into a sitting position. The room spun, and his stomach lurched, so he squeezed his eyes shut until the nauseating sensation dissipated. "You were planning to dispose of my body in the creek?"

"What?" Alice's eyes widened. "No, of course not. The creek would have healed you."

"And dead bodies float. If we were trying to get rid of you, there are plenty of other places where no one would ever think to look."

"Megan!" Alice glared at her friend.

"What?" Megan shrugged. "He asked."

Alice sighed before turning to him. "How's your head?"

"Sore, but crashing full-speed into a closed door will do that."

"Sorry." She picked up the cushion that had been beneath his head and set it on a chair. "I couldn't let you leave with my crow."

"*Your* crow?" He rose to his feet and rested a hand on the wall to steady himself. The throbbing in his temples intensified, making his vision blur again. He needed to sit down and rest, but first, he needed answers. He could only think of one way a magicless warlock could absorb the power of another.

The missing amulet. "What happened exactly?" he asked.

"Umm…" She pressed her lips together, cutting her gaze to Megan before continuing, "I was hoping you could tell me. You're the warlock. How did you steal my crow?"

"I didn't…" He squeezed his eyes shut as his stomach lurched again, and Alice took his arm, guiding him into the chair. Her touch was gentle, and it made his pulse race. If his head didn't feel like it was about to explode, that might have been a good thing.

"Can I get you some water?"

"No, I'll be fine." He glimpsed his bag lying empty on the floor. *Oh, crap. Marty.* "Where's my familiar?"

"You mean that smelly little mongoose who tried to motorboat my bestie?" Megan grabbed a ceramic jar from the floor, and Marty's angry squeal echoed from inside.

Donovan held in a groan. "That would be the one."

Megan thrust the jar toward him. "He wanted to eat you, so we put him in here."

"I let him out," Alice said, "but he scratched up my arm and crawled down my shirt."

"After he stunk up the whole store." Megan crossed her arms.

"My apologies. Marty has always had a flatulence issue." He unlatched the lid and cracked it open to find his familiar's beady eyes glaring back at him. "Go directly into the satchel."

He poked his head out of the jar. "But she—"

"We'll discuss your version of the story later." Donovan lifted Marty from the jar and slipped him into the bag, latching it shut. Marty growled and then let one rip. The flap fluttered as a puff of foul stench escaped, filling the room this time with the scents of sour milk and mold. Every fart from the gassy little mongoose presented a unique bouquet to assault his senses.

Donovan sighed. "I should know not to take him out in public."

"Or at least carry some air freshener." Megan sprayed something into the room that morphed the scent into a light and floral fragrance before she propped open the door.

Now, about Alice's crow... Never, in all his dealings with the supernatural, had a spell been forced upon him like that. Well, there was that one time in seventh grade when Matthias turned him into a slug because his girl-friend had flirted with him, but he tried not to think about the incident. All the slime and the lack of bones... *Disgusting.*

The amulet would have allowed him to take Alice's magic and morph into her crow, but it was no longer in his possession.

Perhaps it was in hers...

"Please, Alice. Can you explain what you meant about the bird I was transformed into being *your* crow? Did you force your magic on me?"

Alice held his gaze, her green eyes boring into him as if she were looking into his soul. "No, I did not. Somehow, you yanked my other self out of my body and used her magic to shapeshift." She crossed her arms. "And I don't appreciate it one bit."

"You didn't happen to go scavenging west of town last night, did you?"

She scoffed. "Why would I be there? There's nothing but forest and fields to the west." Her voice took on a nervous tremble. "I also don't appreciate the accusation in your tone."

Forest, fields, *and* his new house, but he could see it was time to drop the subject. He'd scared her. The last thing he wanted was for this gentle, mysterious woman to be afraid of him. "Of course. My apologies." Accusing her of theft when he had no proof wouldn't get him anywhere. There were a few other possible explanations he should explore first. And he could get to know the intriguing woman while he did it.

Standing—and doing his best to ignore the stabbing pain in his skull—he took her hand, holding it between both of his. "I promise you, I did not steal your crow. That shift in magic must have come from a spell. Do you have any enemies?"

She looked at her hand sandwiched between his, her lips parting slightly as she tugged from his grasp. "Aside from the occasional bear trap, no."

"You know…" Megan wagged her finger between them. "You two have had some explosive chemistry since the moment you walked through the door."

"Megan…" Alice whispered through clenched teeth as Donovan fought his smile. At least he wasn't the only one who sensed the connection.

"I'm just saying, maybe because you are so into each other, it triggered some kind of magical bond."

"I don't…" A pink blush spread across her cheeks as she shook her head.

"I suppose that's possible. It's not unheard of for a warlock's magic to go awry when in the presence of a woman who enamors him." Of course, that was *impossible* for him, due to the fact he had no magic to speak of.

"And sometimes shifters are born with extra powers." Megan moved next to Alice, resting a hand on her arm. "It's not *unheard of* for one of us to inherit a little extra oomph if we have any witches or warlocks in our ancestry."

He arched a brow. This situation—this woman—was becoming more and more fascinating. "Do you have witch ancestry, Alice?"

Her eyes widened briefly every time he spoke her name. "I might…" She sighed. "Okay, yes. I do. This *might* have happened before, but it's not something I can control." She cast her gaze to the floor. "I'm sorry I accused you. I was embarrassed."

"Intriguing. Unharnessed magic is nothing to be ashamed of." And he much preferred that explanation over the alternative.

He glanced at his watch. Of course, he had a conference call with a client in half an hour, but he wasn't finished with Alice yet. "I would love to explore this further, but I have to leave. Will you have dinner with me tomorrow night?"

"Me?" Alice pressed a hand to her chest.

"Well, he's certainly not talking to me," Megan said. "He hasn't taken his eyes off you since he stepped through the door."

Her cheeks reddened again as she drew her bottom lip between her teeth, and his stomach fluttered. He couldn't recall a time he'd ever been so taken by a woman.

"Sure. I'd like that." She turned toward the counter and scribbled something on the back of a business card. "Here's my number. I live in the apartment upstairs."

He took the card and smiled. "I'll pick you up at seven."

"Okay." She lifted a hand and wiggled her fingers. "See you then."

He positioned the bag with his unruly familiar onto his shoulder and strode out the door.

CHAPTER FIVE

"Oh, my gods, Alice!" Megan gaped as Donovan disappeared down the street. "Way to turn on your feminine charm. Seriously, that man was eating out of the palm of your hand."

"Oh, please." Alice fought her grin, but it was no use. Her lips curved up like a bow that refused to be unstrung. "He only asked me to dinner because he wants to figure out how I turned him into a crow."

"Sure. Keep telling yourself that." Megan returned the jar that had held the mongoose to a shelf. "Maybe I should sanitize this before we try to sell it. That was one stinky rodent."

"Good idea." Alice straightened the pieces that were knocked aside during Donovan's lopsided attempt at flight. "He was kind about the whole ordeal, wasn't he? I mean, he looks like he comes from money...intimidating...almost scary. But he seems sweet now that we've met him."

"And he asked you to dinner. What are you going to wear?"

"Definitely not this amulet." She pulled the offending object from her shirt. "I can't believe we made up that story. I don't have any witch ancestry."

"Well, you were flopping around like a perch on a pier when he asked you about being at Rainecourt Manor last night. I was trying to help you out."

"And I appreciate it." She was truly sorry she accused him of stealing her crow, and she did do it because of embarrassment. At least she hadn't lied about that. But she was embarrassed not from untamed magic but because she'd gone dumpster diving in Mr. Hottie's trash can. What would he think of her if he knew?

Nothing good, that's for sure. "Do you think this is what he lost?"

Megan screwed her mouth up to one side as she eyed the pendant. "Doubtful. Unless you didn't really find it in the trash."

"Of course it was in the trash. I didn't steal it."

"You can tell me if you did. I know what's it like when the animal takes over. Sometimes logic flies out the window, and we find ourselves ensnared in instinct...or a trap." She winked.

"You are never going to let me live that down, are you?"

"Probably not."

"Well, I cross my heart I found this necklace in the garbage can outside." She examined the chipped stone. "I should return it to him, though. Just in case."

"Okay." Megan nodded and sprayed Lysol into the jar before attaching the lid and returning it to the shelf. "You can give it to him at dinner...and explain why you were on his property, spying on him in his home and digging through the trash. That won't be embarrassing *at all*."

Alice groaned. She couldn't just hand it to the man and tell him she'd lied to his face after the cover-up story they'd fabricated. There was something about him…something that piqued her crow's interest, making her want to know him. Her crow had never been interested in a man before. She couldn't chance blowing it on their first date. "What am I going to do with it, then?"

"Throw it away? He tossed it in the garbage first. It'll go to the same landfill whether it arrives with your trash or his."

"That doesn't seem right. If, on the off chance he *accidentally* threw it away, and this is what he's looking for, I should return it. I'll fly it back to his house and drop it on his balcony."

"Sure, that could work…unless he sees you."

"Why would it matter if he sees me? Our auras don't glow in animal form, and there are plenty of non-shifting crows in the area. He won't know it's me."

"Alice, dear…" Megan tilted her head. "He seems like a smart guy. Chances are he knows what that amulet is capable of. He knows you're a crow shifter, and he saw a crow on his balcony last night. He already suspected it was you until our little fib saved you. Don't you think he'll put the pieces together?"

Megan had a point. Damn it, she hated when her bestie was right about stuff like this. Donovan may not have gotten a good look at her crow last night, but Farty Marty sure did. "You're right. I should throw it away."

"Maybe…" Her brows lifted as she grinned. "But aren't you curious to see if you can get it to work again? Maybe it wasn't the amulet at all, and y'all's chemistry really did cause the power flip."

"I am pure shifter. If I caused it, the amulet was the reason."

"I know, but don't you want to try flipping the bird to someone else? For science?" Her grin widened, and she wiggled her eyebrows. "Like maybe to your best friend who's always wanted to fly?"

"Hmm…" Alice held up her hand and slowly lifted her middle finger. "How's that?"

Megan pursed her lips. "Cute."

"I am what I am."

"C'mon. Just once? For me?"

"I suppose it wouldn't hurt to give it another try before I toss it. But just this once, and then it goes in the garbage like he intended it to." She took off the necklace and shoved it into her purse. "After we close, we'll go out by the creek, nowhere near his property. If Donovan's attempt at flight is any indicator, you'll need a dip in the stream when you're done."

"Yes!" Megan bounced on her toes. "You're the best, Alice. This is why I love you."

"We've been searching for two hours, boss. I don't think it's out here." Marty's voice had taken on a whining tone that grated on Donovan's nerves. "Can't we go inside? I'm hungry."

"It has to be here." Donovan ground his teeth, which didn't help the tension headache reaching from the base of his skull up to his temples. He crouched on his hands and knees on the lawn outside the manor, running his fingers through the grass, leaving no blade unturned.

Alice had piqued his interest in a way no woman had

ever done, and he suspected she was part of his destiny the seer spoke of. Now, more than ever, he needed to find the damn amulet and fulfill the prophecy before it was too late.

Marty scampered toward him and rose onto his back legs. "You threw away a lot of junk when we first got here. It's probably at the garbage facility."

"I refuse to believe that," he snapped, and his familiar flinched. Donovan continued his search, his heart rate picking up speed as his movements became more frantic. *I dropped it in the yard. I know I did.*

"You don't have to bite my head off." Marty crossed his little arms. "It might be with the trash, whether you believe it or not."

Donovan's nostrils flared as he blew out a breath and sat on the ground. Grass stains marred the knees of his jeans, and dirt clung to his palms. "I apologize, Martin. I don't mean to take out my frustration on you."

"You can find another magic-stealing artifact. That can't be the only one in existence."

"It took me seven months to locate and acquire the amulet. If another exists, I don't have time to find it. I turn thirty-five next month, and then it will all be over. I'll remain a stain on the Rainecourt family name for eternity." And he would finally have to admit he was indeed a failure like his father always believed.

"You're scrappy. You'll think of another plan." Marty fisted his paws and made boxing motions, hopping around like he was in the ring.

Donovan tried to laugh, but he couldn't force any humor into it. "It is my luck Shift Creek sends their refuse to Austin, the first city in this state with a waste-to-energy practice. If I accept the amulet was accidentally thrown away, I must admit it was incinerated. I refuse to give up this quest."

Marty climbed into his lap. "We can go back. The place stank like rotten eggs and rancid meat, but I'll crawl through the garbage and look for it."

He arched a brow. "I would think you'd be used to those scents by now."

"Why would I be used to stink?" Marty looked perplexed. The poor little guy had no idea the effect his irritable bowels had on others.

"There is no garbage left. The attendant showed me the incinerator when we were there. Everything that was picked up this morning was inside, being burned to ash." He stroked Marty's coarse fur, scratching him behind the ear.

"We've scoured the yard. Can I please have a snack now?"

"All right." He set the mongoose on his shoulder and rose to his feet. "How about some grapes?"

"I prefer beef jerky."

Donovan took Marty inside and made him a plate of grapes with a stick of jerky. Sliding into a chair at the breakfast table, he drummed his fingers on the wood while Marty ate. "Are you sure Alice didn't have the amulet this morning? Perhaps she didn't steal it, but if I did accidentally throw it away, she may have found it in the garbage can or lying in the grass outside."

He wanted to believe her story that she had witch ancestry and the magical affront had happened to her before. But with the amulet out of his possession, he couldn't help but suspect.

"I didn't see it anywhere," Marty said.

"Not even when you were down her shirt?"

He shook his head. "It all happened so fast. I was trying to save you from her. I didn't mean to slide into her shirt. It was so crazy, I don't even remember it all." He shoved an entire grape into his mouth, his cheeks puffing out as he stared out the window.

"And you're certain the crow she turned me into wasn't the same crow you tried to have for dinner last night?"

It took a few minutes for the mongoose to chew the grape, but he finally swallowed and wiped his paws down his face. "The crow she turned you into had a patch of white feathers beneath its wing. I didn't see anything but black feathers on the one last night."

"If she has the amulet, and I can convince her to return it, my problems will be solved."

"She doesn't have it, boss. Even if she did, she wouldn't know how to use it. It's not like it came with an instruction manual." He tilted his head. "Or did it?"

"No, it did not, but if she'd had time to research it... I suppose it's possible she figured it out and was trying to steal my magic, and since I have none available to steal, she somehow gave me hers."

"Seriously?" Marty scoffed. "That's a stretch."

Donovan fisted his hands. "You're right. Alice doesn't seem like the menacing type. I can't imagine such a gentle creature trying to take another person's magic. She's far too kind."

Marty narrowed his eyes. "How can you be so sure of her character when you've known her all of fifteen minutes?"

He flattened his palms on the table. "I can't explain it, but it feels like I've known her my entire life."

Marty took a bite of jerky and spoke around the beef in his mouth. "That's ridiculous."

Two days ago, Donovan would have agreed. But the moment he saw the alluring crow shifter, something inside him changed, and he couldn't wait to explore it. "Perhaps she activated the amulet accidentally."

"She doesn't have it, boss. For real."

He sighed. "No, I suppose not. The artifact requires vocalization of intent for the magic to initiate. Why on earth would she say I could have her crow?"

"She wouldn't." Marty crawled across the table and rested a paw on Donovan's hand. "The amulet is gone, boss. It's time for plan B."

Donovan nodded. His hope that Alice might have the amulet dissolved, but he wouldn't give up without a fight. "I must find another artifact."

Alice set her purse on the grass. She'd tucked the amulet inside so she could talk to Megan about "flipping her the bird" without accidentally flipping before she was ready. Honestly, she had no idea how the amulet worked, but she didn't want to take chances with her best friend. Flying could be tricky, especially for someone without it in their blood.

"You'll feel resistance from the air when you flap your wings. Use that to gain lift."

"When I flap *your* wings." Megan shook her arms, rolling her shoulders as if getting ready to exercise.

"That's what I said."

"No, you said when I flap *my* wings. It'll be my mind inside your crow, so they're still your wings."

Alice shook her head. "I'm starting to think the one-fingered bird is all you deserve. You really are impossible."

"I'm sorry. Please flip me the real bird." She batted her lashes. "You know you love me."

Alice sighed and mumbled, "Impossible."

Megan flapped her arms. "Like this?"

"It'll feel different with wings. Make sure you flap both evenly, or you'll end up like Donovan and take a nose-dive." Alice grinned. Where would he be taking her for dinner tomorrow? He was from out of town, so he wouldn't know his way around. Hopefully he wouldn't suggest her parents' place.

She chewed the inside of her cheek, her stomach sinking. He probably would, seeing as how it was the only restaurant with table service in town. Her mother's prying gaze would bore into her back all night if they went there…

"Earth to Alice." Megan waved a hand in front of her face, drawing her from her thoughts. "Are we doing this or not?"

"Sorry. I got lost in my mind for a minute there." She tugged the necklace from her purse.

"Thoughts of a rich, handsome stranger, I suppose?"

"He's technically not a stranger anymore. He had my crow. That's very intimate, if you think about it." He'd had a part of her essence. He'd *been* a part of her.

"Friendly intimate, right?" Megan's lip curled. "Not like sexual intimate? Because I love you, but not like that."

She rolled her eyes and slipped the amulet around her neck. "Don't fly anywhere near Rainecourt Manor, okay?"

"Yes, ma'am."

"Are you ready?"

"Oh, yeah." Meg rubbed her palms together.

"Okay then. You can have my bird."

The amulet heated against Alice's skin, and the same

electric sensation shot through her limbs. As Megan transformed into the crow, Alice dropped to the ground on all fours, her vision growing sharper in the darkness. The moon suddenly seemed twice as bright, and as she lifted her hands in front of her face, she found tiny black paws instead.

Megan, she tried to say, but the sound came out as chittering. *Holy mother of trash pandas.* Alice hadn't just flipped her friend the bird; they'd traded magic.

She looked at Megan in crow form, and Megan cawed before flapping her wings and taking to the air. Unsteady at first, she tumbled through the sky, spiraling toward the ground before righting herself at the last minute and soaring upward.

She better not mess up my feathers. Alice sat on her haunches and watched her friend fly circles around the field. Wrapping her paw—Megan's paw—around a tuft of grass, she yanked it from the ground. *Nice.* Having hands while in animal form sure would be convenient.

Nah. Alice preferred her wings, and it seemed her bestie enjoyed them too. Megan's caw echoed across the creek as she soared back toward her, but she didn't land. She just kept circling and circling, while Alice got more and more impatient.

She made raccoon noises at her friend, but her voice wasn't very loud, and either Megan didn't hear her, or she ignored her completely...probably the latter. Shifting to human form was tempting, but since she didn't know how the magic worked, she didn't dare.

With her luck, she'd traded human forms too. Or worse, she'd get stuck. Who knew?

So she waited. And waited. And waited. Finally, after a million excruciating minutes, Megan attempted a landing.

Of course, her inexperience made her overshoot her target. Her feet hit the ground, but her body kept going, and she tumbled twice before skidding to a stop on her belly.

It was time Alice got her bird back, but... *Oh no.* In animal form, the amulet had been absorbed into her body by the magic. Would it even work if it technically didn't exist? She had to try.

Alice waddled toward her friend and focused on swapping forms. Nothing happened. She vocalized her intent, but since she couldn't form words, the magic didn't respond. It appeared the amulet's power worked via the spoken word, and she could only speak in human form.

She had no choice but to shift and hope for the best. With a deep inhale, she closed her eyes and imagined herself human, in her own body. Her skin tingled, and as the transformation began, her body grew until she found herself on her hands and knees in the dirt. She stood, dusting off her legs, and sighing with relief at the sight of her own knee-high boots.

"Give me back my bird." The electrical zap reversed, and the moment she felt her bird return, she shifted, taking to the air herself and circling above the creek before returning to the ground.

"Ow. I should have asked you how to land before we did this." Megan rubbed her neck. "How'd I do? Better than your boyfriend, that's for sure."

"You did great. Do you need to get in the creek?" Alice settled on the ground next to her.

"Nah. I'll be fine." She looked her up and down. "You took my raccoon. It's okay. I trust you with her, but I wish you'd have told me first."

"I didn't know that would happen." Alice lay on her back, lacing her fingers behind her head and gazing up at the stars. "I did the same thing as when I flipped it to Donovan, but this time, your magic flipped to me too."

"And his didn't?"

"I don't know. If it did, I didn't notice. I was in shock at the time."

"Man, you could have had mad warlock powers for a minute or two, and you didn't even realize it." Megan lay next to her like they did when they were kids after Alice had been grounded for venturing out to dumpster dive with her late at night. Crows weren't naturally nocturnal, and her parents didn't appreciate her adventurousness when she was young.

"Maybe I shouldn't throw away the amulet just yet. I think we might need to do some more research with it."

Megan cut her a sideways glance and grinned. "I agree one hundred percent. At least let me master my landing before you do."

"I'll talk to Donovan tomorrow night and see if I can get him to elaborate on what he lost. If it's not the amulet, I see no need to worry about it, do you?"

"Absolutely not," Megan said. "Any trash is fair game as long as we don't trespass, disturb anyone, or make a mess to find it. The judge said so himself." She rolled onto her side to face her friend, propping her head in her hand. "And no one owns the sky."

"I'll drink to that." Alice pushed to a sitting position. "Wanna grab a bottle of wine and help me pick out an outfit for tomorrow?"

"I thought you'd never ask."

CHAPTER SIX

"The brown jacket goes better with your bag, if you're trying to impress her." Marty spiraled up the bedpost and perched on top.

Donovan ran the lint roller over his dark blue lapel as he eyed his familiar's reflection. He hated to hurt the little guy's feelings, but… "I'm not taking the bag tonight."

"Going for the outdoor dining experience, then? That can be romantic. I'm not going on a leash, though. I'll sit at your feet, and you can pass me scraps under the table."

He slipped on his watch and turned to face the mongoose. "You're not going."

Marty laughed. "Funny. What restaurant did you choose? I think I'm in the mood for chicken."

Donovan arched a brow. "You realize she's a bird shifter, right? I don't think poultry is the best option."

"Meh. She's a crow. Crows'll eat anything."

He lifted the familiar into his arms, carrying him out of the bedroom and closing the door. "I meant it when I said you're not going, Martin. Now, can I trust you roaming free in the house, or should I lock you in your room?"

Marty climbed onto his shoulder and circled around the back of his neck. "But I go everywhere with you."

"Not on dates."

"Sometimes…"

Donovan sighed and plucked the mongoose from his shoulder, setting him on a bench in the hall. "This woman is special. We have such a strong connection, it feels almost magical. That may be the only magic I'll ever experience without the help of an artifact."

"Don't say that, boss. You'll unlock your powers."

"The creek certainly didn't work. For either of us." He and Marty both took a dip in the shallow water beneath the nearly full moon last night. Unfortunately, the creek saw him as nothing more than a human and didn't bring out his magic. "I'd hoped it would at least heal your irritable bowel problem."

"My bowels aren't irritable. There's nothing to heal, and anyway…" He latched onto Donovan's pantleg and climbed back to his shoulder. "The full moon's not for a few more days. That's when it will be strongest."

"You're right, my friend. I must be patient. I may have located an artifact that can help, so if I can acquire it, all will be well."

"You said it would take months. When did you find it? *How* did you find it so fast?"

"While you were out foraging in the woods, I searched through the deepest, shadiest recesses of the dark web. I found a warlock of questionable character bragging in a forum about using an enchanted trowel to drain a fairy of her magic when she refused to make a banshee beautiful."

Marty cringed. "That's harsh. Why'd he need a banshee to be pretty?"

"It seemed the ghoulish harbinger was the only person capable of loving him, but he wasn't capable of looking past her outward appearance."

"Are you sure you wanna do business with a guy like that?"

No, he did not want to do business with a man like that, but what choice did he have? Donovan may have been blessed with good looks, but anyone who saw past his appearance and fake aura would find a dud. He simply wanted his inside to match his outside.

"I've sent him a message to begin negotiations. The trowel lacks the ability to harness the magic it drains, but I'm sure I can locate a bottling artifact to contain it. The process won't be as simple as the amulet would have made it, but it's possible."

Marty made a mewling sound in his throat...his sound of disapproval.

"What is it?"

"Nothing, boss. I just..." He clamped his little mouth shut.

Donovan sat on the bench and placed the mongoose in his lap. "If you see a flaw in my plan, tell me now."

He wiped his paws down his face. "Well, it's just a thought, but... Alice said the creek doesn't reverse flow anymore, right? So, if you take its magic, and it can't regenerate, won't it be gone for good? Kaput?"

"I suppose that's a possibility, but it's a chance I'm willing to take."

"Won't that upset Alice?"

He let out a long, slow breath. Yes, it would upset her, but once he unlocked his magic, he could make it up to her. "Taking the power from the creek is my destiny. You heard the seer's prophecy. Once my mission is complete, I can be the man Alice thinks I am. I can give her anything she wants."

"You're right. That's what you have to do. I'll keep looking in all the nooks and crannies for the amulet, just in case it's still here. It sounds a lot easier than the shovel method."

"Stay indoors. There are wolves and foxes in this area, and neither—shifter or not—would hesitate to have you for a midnight snack."

"Aye-aye, Captain." Marty gave him a mock salute and jumped down onto the bench. "But be careful with the crow woman. I'm not convinced what she did to you was an accident."

"I can't imagine anything she'd have gained from doing it on purpose."

"Still."

He patted the mongoose's head. "I'll be careful. Don't wait up."

Donovan left Marty in the hall and went outside to climb into his rented Audi. The drive into town lasted a mere ten minutes, and he had to circle the block a few times so he didn't arrive early. As much as Alice infatuated him, he didn't want to appear too eager.

At 6:59, he parked on the curb in front of her art gallery/apartment and popped a breath mint into his mouth before strolling around the car to the front door. He rang the bell and slipped his hands into his pockets, stepping back to peer at the window above. The light dimmed moments before the door swung open. It seemed Alice was eager too, and the thought made him smile.

"Are all warlocks this punctual? It's seven o'clock on

the dot." She wore a pewter-colored dress that hugged her feminine curves and a pair of black knee-high boots that drew his gaze to her shapely legs. Her shiny dark hair spilled around her shoulders, and a light coat of makeup accented her vivid green eyes.

He'd never encountered a creature of such beauty... with a smile so disarming. The simple curve of her lips was enough to render him speechless, and the strange bond he felt with her deep in his bones couldn't be denied.

She closed the door behind her, turning the key in the lock before tilting her head at him. "Is everything okay?"

He blinked, his senses returning to him. "You look stunning. Thank you for accompanying me this evening." He offered his arm, and she slipped her hand into the crook of his elbow.

"My pleasure. You look nice too."

He opened the car door, waiting for her to settle inside before closing it and walking around to the driver's side to join her.

"So..." She buckled her seatbelt. "I probably should have asked you some questions before I got in the car. Actually, I should have asked before I agreed to go out with you. That wasn't very smart of me. You could be a psycho for all I know."

He smiled. "Perhaps you felt the strong connection between us and knew in your heart that I'm not."

"Maybe. Or perhaps your chiseled jawline and mysterious dark eyes distracted me, temporarily shutting down the rational part of my brain."

"Hmm... I suppose that could have happened. I do have that effect on people, so I'm told."

She laughed. "I bet you do."

"What would you like to know? I'm an open book."

She twisted in her seat to face him. "We could start with last names. Mine is Crawford."

"And mine is Drake. Anything else before we're on our way?"

"Donovan Drake." She nodded. "That's got a nice ring to it. Can I call you Donny?"

"Not if you expect me to answer."

"That's fair. Where are you from? I can tell by your accent it's not Texas."

He turned toward her. "New York. Upstate originally, but I moved to the city as an adult."

Her brow furrowed briefly, as if she were confused, and she pulled her bottom lip between her teeth in the sensual way she'd done yesterday. His gaze lingered on her mouth, and he couldn't tear it away.

After a moment, she pressed her lips together and nodded. "I can recommend some restaurants in the town over if you haven't decided on a place yet."

"I thought we'd stay local so I can get to know the intriguing crow shifter in her natural habitat."

She gritted her teeth. "Are you talking about The Crow's Nest?"

"Is it not good?"

"Oh, it is, but…it's actually *my* nest. Well, I don't live there anymore, but my parents own the place. I grew up in the apartment upstairs." Wariness tightened her eyes, her face pinching as if the thought of dining in her parents' restaurant was the last thing she wanted to do.

"I see. Too soon to meet the family, then." He winked.

"Way too soon. I don't want you to witness a murder on our first date."

"A murder?" He cocked his head, perplexed. Would

they kill her for bringing him there, or him for daring to date their daughter?

She nodded. "Happens every time we get together."

"Oh, a murder of *crows*." He laughed and started the engine. "Then I'm afraid the burden of choosing a restaurant lies with you. I've only been in town a few days, and I haven't ventured outside the Shift Creek city limits."

"How do you feel about beef?"

"I enjoy a good steak every now and then."

"Oh, this is way better than steak. Head down Center Street, and make a right on the highway."

CHAPTER SEVEN

"If anyone invites you over for barbeque, and they cook burgers and hotdogs on a gas grill, they're not true Texans." Alice reached for the door, but Donovan grabbed it first, holding it open and gesturing for her to enter.

"I'll keep that in mind if I ever receive an invitation."

A fluttering sensation formed in her stomach as she stepped inside. Donovan followed, placing his hand on the small of her back. She wasn't accustomed to chivalry, and being on the receiving end of it made her downright giddy.

Longhorn Trails Barbeque was her go-to place for authentic Texas cuisine, and since Donovan was a New Yorker, she had a feeling he'd never tried the real deal before. There was nothing quite like it.

"They smoke their briskets for twelve hours here, and the ribs are so tender the meat practically falls off the bone." Her mouth was watering just talking about the deliciousness she was about to introduce him to.

He swept his gaze across the dining room, his eyes

widening as they landed on the massive stuffed longhorn bust hanging above the brick fireplace.

"That's Smokey. He was the owner's beloved pet steer," she said. "He loved that beast so much, when Smokey died, he couldn't bear to part with him. So he hired a taxidermist to preserve him."

Donovan blinked, his lips moving like he was hesitating to speak. Finally, he squared his gaze on her. "You don't find it ironic that a man who earns his livelihood selling beef kept a steer as a pet?"

Huh. "I never thought about it that way. Poor Smokey. I wonder if he could smell his cooked friends on him when he got home?"

"Best not to think about that, I believe."

"Yeah, you're right. Let's get in line." She led him to the left, between a barbed wire fence and the wooden wall, to stand in the queue. The restaurant had to file the barbs down, blunting the sharp tips, when too many customers snagged their clothes on the wire. It was better than snagging their skin, which was what happened to the poor animals that got too close to the fences out in the wild. She mentally added barbed wire to her list of unnecessarily cruel mundy inventions.

"Is this the line to be seated? Should we have made a reservation?" Donovan asked.

"No, silly. This is the line to get our food. I've never been to a barbeque restaurant that had table service. Not if barbeque was their specialty, anyway."

"So it's a cafeteria or a buffet?" He looked puzzled.

"I guess you could call it cafeteria-style." And then her faux pas smacked her like a frying pan to the face. Donovan was dressed in slacks and a sportscoat. She'd worn her favorite dress and boots. He was expecting a romantic dinner date, and she'd brought him to a come-as-you-are casual family dining venue. *Way to go, Cassie Nova. That's how you show your true colors.*

"I'm sorry. I don't know what I was thinking bringing you here. Well, I do actually. I wanted you to get a taste of real Texas, and I forgot about the date aspect of this dinner." And the fact that a wealthy, high-class warlock would probably look down his nose at a place like this.

"You forgot we were on a date?" He fought a grin.

"I didn't forget. I just went into tour guide mode, and… There's a nice tapas restaurant down the road. Why don't we go there?"

"Your instinct was to bring me here, so we'll stay. I'd like to try this infamous cuisine you're so fond of."

"Are you sure?" As the line moved, she shuffled forward. "It's not too late to bail."

"I believe it's your turn." He gestured to the counter, where the server stood waiting for her to order.

Thank heaven she realized her mistake before she ordered the plate of beef ribs she was craving. Eating gooey meat off a bone with her hands would have ensured this would be the last dinner she had with Donovan Drake. She'd have had barbeque sauce smeared from ear to ear by the time she was through. Instead, she ordered the brisket with a side of potato salad. Things she could eat with a fork.

Donovan ordered the same, and they carried their trays to a quiet back room. At least she could get the man away from the crowd and the family with five screaming kids under the age of ten. Hopefully she could salvage what was left of the chemistry between them.

They settled at the table, and she dove right into her food, her mind inconveniently blanking when she should have been having a conversation with the smoldering man sitting across from her.

A tangy, smoky crust coated the edges of the meat, and it practically melted on her tongue. She watched Donovan take his first bite, his eyebrows rising as he nodded his approval. "This is very good." He took another bite. "I've had brisket before, but never like this. It's delicious."

The tension in her shoulders eased. "I'm glad you like it. Texans would probably call the brisket you've had a pot roast."

"I suppose they would."

They ate in silence for a few minutes—which felt weird at first because Alice was a notorious chatterbox—but the energy between them, the connection he'd mentioned, made the silence comfortable after a while.

They'd run out of food to fill their mouths soon enough, though, and there was one question he needed to answer before she slipped and revealed she knew too much about him already. "Where are you staying while you're in town?"

He sipped his iced tea, watching her over the rim of the glass, and her pulse thrummed. Was it the sexy man making her feel this way or the thought that he might already know she was the crow who dropped a bomb on his familiar?

Oh, lord, I didn't think about that! It would be bad enough if he figured out she'd been on his balcony. But if he discovered what she'd done to Marty, she'd be MoBAR —mortified beyond all recognition.

"Rainecourt Manor," he finally said. "Are you familiar with the place?"

She swallowed hard. "I've, uh...flown over it a few times. Never gotten a close look, though. Is it nice?"

"Very." He wiped the corner of his mouth with a napkin. "You've never gotten close enough to say...perch on the balcony railing?"

Shit on a shingle! He knew. *More like shit on a mongoose. Ugh!* She had to deny she'd been there. It was the only way to keep her dignity intact. She'd never be able to look him in the eyes again, otherwise. "Heck no. I've never been that close. That would be trespassing, which is illegal, and I don't do illegal things." *Anymore.*

He grinned, giving her a curious look. Did he believe her?

"What?" She widened her eyes innocently. *Please let him believe me.*

"It's not every day you hear a grown woman use the word *heck*." He winked. "Do you ever cuss?"

She let out a breath. He must've believed her if he dropped the subject like a hot potato. *Thank my lucky stars.* "Oh, I do. Just not the word you'd normally use in place of heck."

"Why not?" His dark eyes were intense as he held her gaze, like he was actually interested in the reason for her word choice. She wasn't used to a man being this interested in her, especially not a man like Mr. Hottie here.

Her throat thickened. Why the heck was her throat thickening? And was that sweat forming on her palms? *Jeez Louise. Chill, woman.* She cleared her throat. "About fifteen years ago, my cousin accidentally summoned a demon with a spirit board."

He blinked twice. "That's not good."

"Nope, it wasn't. It made her do some freaky stuff." She shuddered at the memory. "Three exorcisms later, she was fine, but she made me swear never to take the name of

H-E-double-hockey-sticks or the big guy who runs it in vain. So, 'heck' it is."

Of course, saying the word wouldn't actually invoke the devil, but why take chances? Besides, she was used to making substitutions for it these days. It would take a major shit-show of a situation for her to even *think* the real one now.

"Interesting." He smoothed his napkin in his lap. "Well, I'm glad to hear you've never been to the manor. Marty tried to eat a crow on the balcony the other night, and if it was you, I wanted to apologize."

Dammit. So much for dropping it like it's hot. "It wasn't me."

He nodded, seemingly satisfied. "I'd be happy to give you a tour sometime if you're interested. It's a beautiful estate."

"Oh. Yeah, that would be great." She shoveled a mound of potato salad into her mouth. He wouldn't be offering her a tour if he knew she'd already been there, right? Right! Whew! Crisis averted.

Sure, she'd regret lying to him later. Or maybe she wouldn't. Maybe, months from now—if they were still together—she could say, "Remember when…" and they'd both have a good laugh. Maybe he'd have a funny secret to tell her too. Wouldn't that be a hoot?

She ate a few more bites before her stomach felt on the verge of popping like an over-inflated balloon. Also, not the smartest thing to do on a first date, but what could she say? The pickings in Shift Creek were slim, and she didn't get out much. She was out of practice.

"How'd you manage to become the owner of Rainecourt Manor, anyway?"

He paused with the fork halfway to his lips and returned it to his plate. "Who said I'm the owner?"

Holy mother of blunders. She'd done it now. With her hands in her lap beneath the table, she twisted her napkin in clenched fists, desperate to come up with a plausible reason for knowing about the deed that didn't make her sound like a stalker.

Straightening her shoulders, she looked him square in the eyes. "You know how small towns are. The house sat empty for thirty-five years, so when a new tenant showed up, word spread fast."

"Yes, I supposed it did." He sipped his drink, wariness clouding his eyes. "Why did you ask where I was staying if you knew the answer?"

"You already thought I was the bird on your balcony —which I wasn't. I couldn't have you thinking I was some sort of Peeping Tammy, now could I?"

"Is there anything else you already know about me? My family line? My magic?" His voice held an edge she'd never heard before, like someone had slipped a razorblade into the rocky road of his cadence.

It was time she came clean. Not about the spying or what she did to his familiar...there was no need for that now...or ever. Heck, maybe he could even help her find one of the brothers if she told him the truth. "Here's the thing. Shift Creek desperately needs a Rainecourt to return. The creek is drying up because the magic is tied to the family—or so we've been told by the myriad witches we've called in to fix it. I'm on the committee that's trying to find a solution to the problem, so when you showed up in town, I had to find out if you were one of Marcus's sons."

She couldn't stop her lip from curling as she said the

man's name. "I went to city hall to get the scoop, but all anyone knew was your name and that you had the deed to the property. You're not a Rainecourt, and, frankly, I'm glad you're not. I mean, if you were, you could have saved the town, but whatever." She clamped her mouth shut before she said anything else stupid. This date was going so much better before they got out of the car.

He held up a finger. "I want to know more about why you think a Rainecourt can save your town, but first tell me why you're glad I'm not one."

"A Rainecourt wouldn't give someone like me the time of day, much less an evening out."

He narrowed his eyes. "What do you mean 'someone like you'?"

"Someone...average. A bottom-feeder." Was it hot in here? Someone must have cranked up the heat because her cheeks felt like she'd washed her face in jalapeño juice.

Donovan laid his knife and fork parallel on the plate and pushed it aside. "There is nothing average or bottom-feeding about you, Alice."

Straightening her spine, she held his gaze. The man seemed sincere, so why was she letting him ruffle her feathers? *Save face, girl. Get it together and be the strong, confident woman you are.* "Oh, I know I'm fabulous." She tossed her hair behind her shoulder. "I was talking about my animal. Non-predators aren't exactly the most appealing creatures in the shifter world."

"It's a good thing I'm not a shifter then."

She smiled. "I guess it is."

He rested his arm on the table, palm up, and she hoped to high heaven it was an invitation because she placed her hand in his without even thinking. His fingers curled around hers, and heck yeah! That was the first thing she'd done right this evening. She was on a roll now.

"You never answered my question," she said. "How did you come to own the house? Were you friends with Marcus? Do you know his sons?"

The skin around his eyes tightened, and a shadow passed over his features. "I wouldn't call what we had friendship."

Curiosity gnawed in her gut, but she managed to keep her filter in place. He seemed shrouded in a hornets' nest of mystery, and it was time she stopped poking it. "Did you buy the house when Marcus died?"

"It was left to me in his will."

She laughed. "That's surprising."

"How so?"

"I just can't imagine Marcus Rainecourt gifting anything to anyone. He's responsible for the town's slow demise, yet he refused to do a damn thing about it when we asked. Selfish bastard. I hate that man. I'm sure his sons are no better."

Donovan's face took on a strange expression as he straightened. He looked almost hurt—or possibly offended—at her words.

Real smooth, Alice. He must have had some sort of relationship with the Rainecourts to be included in the will, and she just started slinging insults like prison slop. "I'm sorry. Even if you weren't friends, you knew him. I shouldn't say those things about a dead guy...or any guy. It's just...when someone has the power to save your home, yet they refuse, it's hard not to take it personally."

"What could Marcus have done to help?"

"Moved back to Shift Creek. Like I said the creek's magic is tied to his family. The trouble started when he moved everyone away, and it won't end unless someone from the bloodline returns. You don't happen to know how to get in touch with his sons, do you?"

"Sadly, I haven't spoken to either of them in years." He squeezed her hand before releasing his hold.

She immediately missed the warmth of his touch. He had some kind of sordid history with the infamous family, and she was dying to know what went down. But Donovan was turning inward. It was probably best to save that conversation for their second date. And then maybe she could convince him to try and contact one of the brothers. Their dad left him a whole damn house. They must have been close.

"You love your town, don't you?" he asked.

"Well, yeah. It's where I grew up. I love the people, the aesthetic…everything about it. Don't tell anyone, but I have aspirations to be on the city council." Her cheeks warmed again at the admission. Not even Megan knew about that little dream.

"And I suppose it's silly since I'm not actually related to her," she continued, "but the warlock who blessed the creek back in the 1800s married a crow shifter. I feel a sort of kinship, I guess."

His brow rose. "I had no idea the family had shifter blood."

"I don't think any of their descendants mated with shifters, so it's diluted by now. I doubt the current family can shift."

"Fascinating." He reached for her hand again, and she let him take it. Something stronger than mere interest sparked in his eyes. "If a Rainecourt came to town, what would he need to do to save the creek?"

"Good question. Cast a spell, I suppose. Infuse the

creek with healing magic again. Take a swim. Maybe just be here." She lowered her gaze to where his thumb traced circles on the back of her hand and tried her damnedest not to imagine him tracing circles somewhere else on her body. It didn't work.

She cleared her throat. "All we have is an oral history about the blessing of the creek. It's been recorded now, but by the time someone thought to write it down, the first two generations had passed away, so there are some missing pieces to the puzzle."

Okay, that wasn't completely true. A secret, highly detailed written account did exist, but only the town librarian and the people on the save-the-creek committee knew about it. The problem was, the author had enchanted the book so only a Rainecourt could read it.

"I don't know how much luck I'll have," Donovan said, "but I will do my best to get someone from the bloodline to pay the town a visit."

"That would be amazing. If you can pull that off, I won't be able to thank you enough."

"Simply seeing the light in your eyes is all the thanks I need."

Speaking of eyes, with the way he looked at her, it felt like he'd stripped her bare, caressed every inch of her skin, and then moved on to her soul. *Wowzers.*

"You're not just saying that so you'll get lucky tonight, are you?" She arched a brow.

He chuckled. "A gentleman never allows himself to get lucky on a first date."

"Sucks for you."

He licked his lips, and a sly smile curved his mouth. "Good things come to those who wait."

"I've never been very patient." And if he didn't stop

looking at her like that, she might not be able to stop herself from climbing over the table and showing him how *impatient* she really was.

"I suppose our second date should be sooner, rather than later, then."

"Tomorrow's good." She bit her tongue. *Way to sound desperate. Abort! Abort!* "I mean, actually, no, it's not. I've got a dinner thing with my parents." That wasn't a lie. All she had to do was show up, and they'd feed her. Now, she'd just have to be sure she showed up tomorrow night.

"The next night is the full moon. I assume you'll be busy with your committee then?"

"Yeah. Every month, we head out to the source to watch for signs of recovery...or further demise." Her shoulders started to slump, so she straightened them. She was on a date with Mr. Hottie, and he wanted to see her again. Fretting over the creek right now wouldn't do a lick of good.

"How about Monday?" he asked.

"Monday is perfect." She started to take another bite of potato salad but thought better of it. She had one more thing she'd promised to ask him. "You mentioned you'd lost something when you came into the gallery yesterday. Did you ever find it?"

Another strange expression crossed his face. The man was like a knotted ball of yarn she couldn't wait to unravel. "I've found something else that will suffice," he said.

"What did you lose?"

"A trinket. Nothing to be concerned about." Rising to his feet, he offered her his arm. "Shall we?"

She smiled, trying not to look too relieved. "We shall."

He drove her home, pulling up to the curb and killing the engine before turning toward her. "Have you ever considered exploring more of your magic?" His gaze dipped to her mouth briefly.

Hot damn. Maybe he didn't want to be a gentleman after all. "What did you have in mind?" Maybe he was into role-playing. She could be down with that.

"You mentioned you've given someone your crow once before and that you can't control it. I wonder if I could help you? I've studied magic in all its forms extensively."

So not the direction she thought he was headed with that question. "Oh. Yeah, no." She shook her head. "I'm good."

He took her hand. "Aren't you curious to find out what else you can do?"

She was curious to find out what *he* could do, but his mind was obviously not joining hers in the gutter. "It's… painful. It feels like I'm being turned inside out and scrambled with a hand mixer, so I'd really rather not." Okay, the hand mixer was a bit of an exaggeration, but it really did start to hurt after a bit when her crow was outside her body.

"I'm so sorry. I didn't realize it was painful. Perhaps learning to control it…"

"Really, it's okay. Megan was right. Being near you mixes up my hormones, and the sudden attraction caught me by surprise. I lost control for a hot minute, but it won't happen again."

He arched a brow. "I'm certain I could make you lose control again…and again."

Okay, that *had* to be a gutter thought, right? "I can't wait to see you try."

"Indeed." He slipped out of the car and hurried around to open her door before she could even get her seatbelt off. Offering his hand, he helped from her seat and walked her to the front door.

She turned to him, inching closer and looking into his dark brown eyes. "Does a gentleman kiss on the first date?"

His gaze lowered to her lips. "Only if the lady wants him to."

"She does."

Cupping her cheek in his hand, he leaned down, brushing his mouth to hers. His face was freshly shaven, free of stubble, and his lips felt like velvet against hers. When his mouth opened, his tongue teasing her lips apart, she couldn't stop the whimper from escaping her throat.

He placed his other hand on the small of her back, and she went for it, closing the distance between them, pressing her body to his. If she wasn't going to get lucky tonight, he at least needed to know what he'd be missing.

A masculine grunt emanated from his throat as he held her closer, and she let her hands wander over his shoulders, taking in as much sinew as she could through his jacket. The man was built.

With a deep inhale, she broke the kiss, stepping back and tracing a single finger down his chest. "I hope I'm leaving you wanting more."

His eyes smoldered as he grinned. "So much more."

"Good. I'll see you Monday."

CHAPTER EIGHT

Donovan couldn't remember a time when his heart had felt so light. Not only did his date with Alice end with enough heat to burn him to ash, but he'd learned more about his ancestors than his father ever cared for him to know.

Yesterday, he'd made a deal to acquire the magic-bottling artifact, and it was on its way to Texas. The warlock in possession of the enchanted trowel didn't want to part with it, but Donovan had a few tricks up his sleeve. With a little research on the man, he could figure out his desires and find an item that would be a tempting trade.

Now, as he sat at the sidewalk table in front of the coffee shop, waiting for Shifted Treasures to open, the morning sun warmed his face, and he smiled.

"Are you sure this is a good idea?" Marty jumped onto the table and sat upright on his haunches. "Flowers yesterday, and now coffee this morning? Seems desperate to me."

"There's nothing desperate about showing a woman you care."

"There's certainly not," the barista purred as she set a drink holder with three paper cups on the table. She appeared in her mid-fifties, and she wore bright red lipstick and enough perfume to give Marty a run for his money in the stench department. "Here's your order, hon. If it doesn't work out with your girl, I'm available."

"Thank you, ma'am, but I intend to do everything in my power to make it work."

"You know where I am." She winked before turning on her heel, flipping her blonde hair over her shoulder, and strutting inside.

"Now, there's a woman you can sink your teeth into," Marty said. "Why not take her up on her offer?"

Donovan shook his head. "She's a cougar. Both literal and figurative." And probably one of the predator shifters who made Alice feel inferior.

"That's never stopped you before."

He sighed. Perhaps he could locate a female familiar for Marty. If the mongoose had a mate, he might stop trying to convince Donovan to sleep with every woman he saw. In his current magicless condition, he could never identify—much less tame—a wild familiar on his own, but he could contact the dealer his father purchased Marty from...

His hand clenched into a fist at the memory of receiving Marty as a gift when he was fifteen. Familiars should be found, not bought. The "gift" was meant to embarrass more than anything, and Donovan was lucky Marty had accepted his place alongside a warlock with no magic.

He shook his head to get rid of the memory. "My interest lies solely with Alice."

"I don't trust her."

"You don't know her."

"She forced her magic on you." He crossed his arms.

"That was an accident triggered by our undeniable connection."

Marty blew a hard breath through his nostrils. "You don't really believe you've got crow shifter blood, do you? That seems like something you'd have known about."

"My father kept the entire town a secret from me, and I doubt he ever discussed it with my brothers. They weren't even allowed to speak of their mother in his presence."

"But none of them can shift."

"As Alice said, the magic has been diluted over the generations. If my father knew about his lineage, he would not have made it public that his blood was tainted." Alice was right about his family thinking themselves better than a crow. To admit that aspect of their bloodline would have humiliated his father.

"And you still haven't made it public that you're his son." Marty took a huge bite of a blueberry muffin, and crumbs peppered the fur on his face.

Donovan took his coffee from the holder and sipped the bitter, hot liquid. Alice had made her disdain for his family quite clear on their date. He felt guilt, and maybe a little shame, for not telling her who he was, but he couldn't bear to have her dismiss him for a lineage he'd prefer not to claim.

"I will tell her when the time is right."

"When will that be?" He took another bite, his little cheeks puffing out like a chipmunk as he chewed.

"Perhaps when I restore the creek and save the town."

Marty laughed, spewing crumbs across the table.

Donovan narrowed his eyes at his familiar and waited for him to finish.

"Oh, you're serious?" Marty climbed up his arm and perched on his shoulder. "C'mon, boss, don't let a woman make you lose focus. We came here to unlock your magic, and then we're going home. That's the plan."

"Plans change." He plucked the mongoose from his shoulder and returned him to the table. "This town is dying, and I can save it."

"How? You're here. You've swam in the creek every night since we arrived, and it hasn't made any difference."

"Tonight is the full moon. Perhaps my presence on its night of restoration will do the trick."

"Or maybe the creek needs someone who can cast a spell to fix it."

"If my presence tonight doesn't heal it, I will scour the web for an artifact with the power—"

"You could call one of your brothers."

Donovan's teeth clenched with an audible click. "That would be a last resort."

At best, Matthias would laugh and remind him what an incompetent embarrassment he was to the family before refusing to help. Donovan's ears burned at the mere thought of the conversation. Griffin might be willing to offer assistance...*if* Donovan could locate him. But he wasn't sure he could bear the shame.

"You're going to save the town, get the girl, and then unlock your magic?" Marty licked his paws and wiped his face.

"That's the plan."

The mongoose nodded. "Okay. What can I do to help?"

Donovan glanced across the street, where Alice stood

inside her gallery, turning the Closed sign over to read Open. "Get in the satchel and try not to stink up their store."

Alice grinned as she positioned the vase overflowing with flowers on the counter next to the cash register. Donovan surprised her yesterday, having the fragrant bouquet of roses, lilies, and chrysanthemums delivered to her right after lunch. Of course, she'd have preferred to see the warlock himself rather than a delivery driver, but he'd get no complaints from her. She couldn't remember the last time a man sent her flowers.

"Are you gonna carry that thing around with you everywhere until it dies?" Megan leaned on the counter to sniff a lily.

"I thought it looked nice on the counter yesterday, so I brought it down this morning. The apartment and the store hardly qualify as everywhere." And she got giddy every time she looked at it, which was an emotion she'd like to get used to.

"It is pretty," Megan said. "That vase looks like real crystal. It probably cost more than we make here in a week."

"Maybe." She ran her finger over the cut glass.

"Alice has a boyfriend," Megan sang.

"Until he goes back to New York." Alice crossed her arms. She shouldn't allow herself to fall for a man who lived thousands of miles away. Long-distance relationships rarely worked, and she'd sooner apply lipstick to an ornery alligator than leave her home and move into a crowded city.

"Did he say how long he's planning to stay?"

"No. I didn't want to ply him with too many questions. He seems guarded. Kept steering the conversation back to me and the town, and of course, I ate it up."

"Who wouldn't? I'm surprised you didn't eat *him* up."

"Believe me, I wanted to." She tugged the amulet from her pocket. "He didn't mention this when I asked him what he'd lost."

"Did he tell you what he was missing?"

"He called it a trinket that wasn't important and then changed the subject."

Megan shrugged. "Sounds like you're in the clear then. His trash is your treasure."

"I guess so." At the sound of bells chiming, Alice turned toward the door, and Donovan stepped into the store. He carried a tray of drinks in his hands, and his mongoose poked his head from the bag.

"Speak of the devil," Alice said under her breath as she passed the amulet to Megan, who whisked it under the counter before shoving her hands in her pockets. *Whew. That was close.*

"Donovan, what a surprise!" Alice grinned, silently praying he hadn't seen the pass.

He nodded to Megan and winked. "Something you don't want me to see?"

"Oh, umm…" *Crap on a cracker.* Alice widened her eyes at her friend.

"Tampon," Megan said, her own eyes wide and unblinking. "It's my time of the month, see?" She rummaged beneath the counter, most likely in Alice's purse, and pulled out a tampon, waving it in the air. "I'm just gonna go…" Flashing Alice an apologetic look, she disappeared into the back room.

Marty glared at Alice as Donovan set the drinks on the counter and softly kissed her cheek. Why did she get the feeling his familiar didn't like her much?

"Thank you again for the flowers." She glanced at the mongoose, who disappeared into the satchel.

"You're welcome again. I brought you and Megan some coffee to start your day." He removed the drinks from the tray and offered her one.

"That's very sweet." She took a sip. "You'd best be careful, though. A girl could get used to this kind of treatment."

"I hope you do." The skin around his dark eyes crinkled with his smile. "I've got work to do, so I'll be going. I'm looking forward to our date tomorrow night."

"You and me both."

"Have a wonderful day, Alice." He kissed her hand—actually pressed his lips to the back of her hand like a Victorian gentleman—and her heart did flip-flops in her chest.

"You too, Donovan. Bye, Marty."

As Donovan walked out the door, the mongoose either blew raspberries at her or farted, confirming her suspicion. But she wasn't about to let the little weasel come between them.

Donovan would probably sell the estate and move back to New York soon, and she intended to have as much fun with the man as she could until then.

CHAPTER NINE

The full moon hung high in the cloudless sky as Alice swooped down by the springs, landing next to Christine, the head of the save-the-creek committee. Her blonde hair was pulled back in a tight ponytail, and mud clung to her boots as if she'd walked here rather than flown in her hawk form.

Alice shifted to human as Bryan approached from the bushes. Dark brown fur covered his bear's body, and a deep grunt sounded in his throat as he peered at the waning creek. It was almost midnight. The water should have reversed flow hours ago.

"If we don't figure something out soon, the mundies are going to dredge it," Alice said. "They've requested three quotes. One of the companies is supe-run, so I've asked them to stall."

"Good thinking," Christine said. "Where are the humans now?"

"Near the river. They're still convinced the reversal begins where the creek joins it." Of course, the mundies knew nothing about the magical origin. They'd heard the legend, but no one believed it. Instead, they focused on finding a scientific reason for the shift in flow, which had kept them out of the secret supe committee's hair. But now they were taking it too far.

Bryan shifted to human form and kneeled on the bank, peering into the water below. "The level has dropped half a foot from last month. Dredging might be our only option."

Alice scoffed. "It could destroy what little magic is left."

"She's right," Christine said. "We need more time. What did you find out about Donovan Drake? Can he contact the brothers?"

"He's trying. He said he hasn't spoken to them in years, so he might not have much luck either."

"We'll cross our fingers that he does. Bryan, do you have anything to add?"

He rose to his feet. "The warlock I brought in last week confirmed it, and that brings the total to five. The magic is tied to the family, so finding a Rainecourt is our only hope."

Christine nodded. "I'll put another call in to Matthias's firm, relaying our desperation. Alice, continue your search for Griffin and implore Mr. Drake for his assistance."

"I will."

In a cloud of shimmering gold, Christine transformed into her hawk and flew toward town. Bryan followed suit, shifting into bear form and galloping into the brush.

Alice sighed, casting a wistful gaze over the once brimming creek before turning into her crow and taking to the sky. Donovan didn't mention if he'd tried to contact the brothers when she saw him this morning, and his presence always seemed to short-circuit her brain, making her forget to ask. She'd have to text him tomorrow and see if he'd had any luck.

If her beak would have allowed her to smile, she'd have grinned from wing to wing. Just thinking about the man made her stomach flutter like a teenager with her first crush. She should have gone home, but without even thinking about her direction, she found herself flying toward the manor.

A quick circle above wouldn't hurt, as long as she didn't land on the balcony and nearly get eaten this time. But she didn't make it all the way to the house.

Movement at the creek below drew her eye to where Donovan stood on the bank, peering at the water. He peeled his shirt over his head, revealing a delectable six-pack that made her mouth water.

If he was planning a midnight swim, she didn't want to miss it. She silently swooped toward a tree, landing on a high branch where the leaves would obscure her from his view. When he stripped down to his boxer briefs and stepped into the water, Alice clamped her beak shut to keep the excited caw from slipping out.

The man was as gorgeous as she imagined, with defined muscles and firm, smooth skin. The only flaw on his otherwise perfect body was the six-inch crescent-shaped scar on the left side of his chest, but that would soon disappear, thanks to the magical creek.

He waded into the water, which barely reached his waist, before sinking beneath the surface. The sounds of his familiar scurrying beneath the tree barely registered in Alice's mind as Donovan rose to his feet, the moonlight glinting off his gloriously wet, ripped body. His biceps flexed as he ran his hands through his hair, angling his face toward the sky and breathing deeply.

Good gravy. It was like watching a god emerge from the sea.

She shouldn't have stayed there perched in the tree and watching him like a stalker...again. But she couldn't tear her gaze away from all that perfection. Oddly, though he'd been in the water for at least five minutes, the scar on his chest hadn't begun to fade.

She swallowed hard. Either the creek had finally lost its power, or Donovan had been hit with some powerful battle magic at some point in his life. As much as the idea that he'd fought another warlock pained her, she really, *really* hoped that was why he wasn't healing.

"Hey. What are you doing up there?" Marty's nasally voice pierced the silence, and she couldn't stop herself from cawing in response as he climbed the tree. He made it to the first level of branches before leaping—or attempting to leap—toward her.

Alice took to the sky, but Marty missed the branch entirely. He free-fell, bouncing off the lowest bough before landing in the dirt with a thud.

She was tempted to fly home and avoid any chance of a confrontation, but the little guy wasn't moving. He might not have been breathing.

Donovan just stood there, staring at the moon, oblivious to his familiar's predicament, which was weird. As far as Alice knew, familiars and their warlocks had almost telepathic connections, so Donovan should have sensed the mongoose's trouble.

Alice landed on the ground next to Marty and nudged him with her beak. He didn't move. She stared at his chest, waiting to see the rise and fall of his breaths. Nothing.

Oh, crud on a cookie. She couldn't leave him there to die. Letting out a caw, she flapped her wings, trying to get Donovan's attention, but he seemed lost in some trance-like state.

What a craptastic night this has turned out to be. She had no choice but to shift and carry the mongoose into the creek herself. Once in her human form, she kicked off her shoes, cradled the little guy in her arms, and splashed into the water.

"Donovan!"

He blinked, coming out of his meditation and rushing toward her. "Marty! What happened?"

"Get him in the water." She handed the familiar to Donovan, who sank into the stream, dunking Marty completely before lifting his head above the surface.

"Breathe, Marty. Breathe!" He stroked his chest.

"Give it some time. He's a magical being, so the creek should heal him." Her gaze locked on Donovan's scar. "I hope." She could not be the reason he lost his familiar. If Marty made it through, that was the last time she'd ever play Peeping Tammy again. *Please let the little rat be okay.*

"Did you see what happened to him? Was he attacked?"

"He was trying to climb the tree." She pointed at the place she'd been perched.

"Why was he trying to climb the tree? Marty is afraid of heights."

"Because he saw...me." Her ears burned at her admission.

"You?" Donovan gave her a curious look, but before he could say anything else, the familiar sucked in a tiny, mongoose-sized breath. "Marty."

His beady eyes blinked open, his gaze darting between

Alice and Donovan as he recovered fully from his fall. "It was her!" His tiny arms flailed about, splashing in the water until Donovan lifted him to his chest. "She was in the tree, spying. I told you we can't trust her."

"I was not spying." Alice parked her hands on her hips. Marty was a lot nicer when he was unconscious. "And I just saved your life, so you should show a little appreciation." She should have known he'd give her away with his first breath.

"You knocked me out of the tree," Marty accused.

"You jumped and missed the branch while trying to attack me." She crossed her arms. "What do you have against me, anyway?"

"You're a threat to our mission."

"What mission?"

"All right, Martin. You need to calm down. Are you injured?" He placed the mongoose on his shoulder and took Alice's hand, guiding her toward the bank.

"I'm fine," Marty pouted.

"Tell Alice thank you for bringing you into the water. If she hadn't been there, you might still be lying unconscious in the dirt."

"If she hadn't been there, I wouldn't have—"

"Martin…" Donovan's voice held an edge of warning.

"Thank you, Alice," Marty grumbled.

"You're welcome." She clambered onto the shore and grabbed her shoes, slipping them onto her feet. She was soaked from the waist down, and her jeans were already starting to chafe. *Fan-friggin-tastic.*

Donovan set the mongoose on the ground and pulled on his pants. "Go to the house, Marty. I'll be there in a few minutes."

"But…"

"Are you injured in any way?"

"No," he pouted.

"Then don't make me tell you again." He sounded like a father scolding his son.

"Fine." The mongoose scurried through the grass toward the manor, and Donovan turned toward her.

"I apologize for his behavior. I'm afraid he feels threatened by you."

Alice laughed. "As if a crow ever threatened anyone. We're not bad omens, either. That's just superstition."

"He's scared of losing me, should I find a mate." He buttoned his jeans and looked into her eyes, pausing as if giving her time to respond.

A mate? Did he just mention finding a mate? As in a life partner, someone to spend forever with, a wife? *Whoa, Nelly. Don't put the cart before the stallion.* Just because the mongoose was scared it was happening, it didn't mean Donovan was heading in that direction.

She'd only known the man a few days. Then again, shifters did bond quickly when they found a compatible mate—animal instincts and all—and if she were honest with herself, she'd admit her instinct was drawing her to this man like he was the shiniest thing she'd ever seen.

But Donovan wasn't a shifter. As far as she knew, warlocks treated love the same as humans: as a game or a quest. And they didn't have bonding instincts. Best to play it cool.

"Oh, I see." She swept her gaze down the length of him, lingering first on his scrumptious abs and then taking in his scar. That must've been wickedly painful. "And have you...found one?"

He smiled. "I've found potential for the first time in my life."

"Potential." She nodded. *Good answer.* "I think I've found it too."

"I'm glad we're on the same page." Still clutching his shirt in his hand, he closed the distance between them and trailed his fingers down her cheek.

She wasn't sure if it was the cool spring breeze or his touch giving her goosebumps, but when he leaned in to kiss her, warmth unfurled in her chest, cascading downward and settling below her navel.

She glided her hands up his stomach, and he responded by deepening the kiss, wrapping his arm around her lower back and pulling her hips to his. The man was hard…all over. *Holy mother of smoked sausage!*

Leaning into him, she linked her fingers behind his neck and kissed him like she was a diver and he was the last ounce of air in her tank.

As the kiss slowed, he pulled away, his tongue gliding over his swollen lips, and she couldn't help but imagine it caressing another set of lips. Her mind wasn't just in the gutter, it had tumbled down the storm drain, and she wasn't the slightest bit ashamed. The man was sex on a stick. She shivered.

His brow furrowed. "You're soaking wet."

You have no idea.

"Why don't you come to the house? I'm sure I've got a pair of sweatpants you could borrow."

Yes, please. "I can shift and fly home. I don't want to be a bother."

"I don't want you to go home." His eyes were intense, holding her hostage, and she was a willing prisoner.

"You did promise me a tour."

Donovan slipped on his shirt before taking Alice's hand and leading her up the path toward the manor. He fought a smile as he imagined what must have been going through her mind when she found him stripped down to his underwear, wading into the creek.

He couldn't blame her for perching in the tree. If their positions had been reversed, he'd have stopped to watch too. He doubted he'd have kept his presence a secret for as long as she did, though. Being near her, he felt as if he'd found the one thing in this world that could make him whole.

The creek had healed Marty, though it had done nothing for Donovan's magic or his scar. That could only mean the spirit of the stream recognized him as human, and it would never unlock his magic unless he used an artifact to harness its power. His presence had done nothing to reverse the flow, so Alice's theory that a Rainecourt simply being here would solve their problems had been disproven.

As he opened the front door and gestured for her to enter, he made up his mind to set his ego aside and help her in any way he could. A call to Griffin was in order, and he'd make it tomorrow morning.

Marty darted out onto the stair rail, and Donovan cut him a look, jerking his head toward the familiar's room. He blew out a hard breath through his nose, but he took the hint and disappeared down the hall.

"This place is amazing." Alice started toward the grand staircase but paused. "I don't want to drip all over your house. I'd hate to ruin the floors right before you sell it."

"Who says I'm going to sell?"

"I assumed, since your life is in New York, you'd be putting it on the market soon."

Her tongue slipped out to moisten her lips, and his knees nearly buckled. Never in his life had he felt this way about another person. He wanted her, not just in his bed, but in his life. The emotion felt primal, like it came from a part of him deep inside, a part he never knew existed.

Could it be the diluted bit of shifter magic in his blood connecting to hers? Whatever it was, he refused to fight it. "Perhaps I'd like to make a life here. Leave the old one behind."

Perhaps it was no coincidence this manor was the only thing his father left him. Maybe it was fate, or maybe it was simply serendipity. He was here now, either way, and he planned to make the most of it.

"It's a good place to make a life." Her eyes searched his. Did she feel the same connection?

"My extra clothes are upstairs in the bedroom."

She smiled slyly. "But I'm so wet."

Gods have mercy. Blood rushed to his groin, and he held in a groan. "Then we'd better get there quickly." He swept her into his arms, cradling her to his chest, and took the stairs two at time. He couldn't get her out of those wet clothes fast enough.

CHAPTER TEN

The staircase split in opposite directions, and Alice took in the beauty of the home as Donovan carried her to the second floor. He made a right, striding down a wide hallway with plush burgundy carpet and wood paneling on the walls.

It wasn't exactly the tour she'd hoped for, but if he had the same grand finale in mind, she'd be happy to see the rest of the estate later. Right now, she wanted to see more of the delectable man who carried her like she weighed no more than her crow.

As he stepped into the same bedroom she'd seen him in when she perched on the balcony, he lowered her feet to the floor and locked the door. "I think we minimized the damage."

She bit her bottom lip, sweeping her gaze down his form and up to his eyes. "I'm still *very* wet."

He swallowed. "Would you like me to get you some clothes?"

"That depends. Are you still being a gentleman?"

"Do you want me to be?"

"Absolutely not." She peeled her wet shirt over her head and dropped it on the dresser. The entire room looked expensive, and she knew first-hand how smelly carpet could get when you left something wet on it overnight.

And the plans she had for him would take all night.

"That makes two of us." He took off his shirt and laid it next to hers before wrapping his arms around her and kissing her.

His hands roamed up and down her back, gliding along her bra before he unhooked it. The garment hung from her shoulders as he held her close, and he slid his fingers into her hair, brushing his tongue to hers.

She slipped off her bra, tossing it aside—it was mostly dry so no harm done to the rug—and she kneaded his firm shoulders as she moaned into his mouth.

"Alice." His voice was raspy and deep, reminding her again of rocky road ice cream, and she couldn't wait to taste him.

She unbuttoned his pants, working them over his hips before peeling his underwear—still wet from the creek—down his legs. After toeing off his shoes, he stepped out of his clothing and stood before her, gloriously nude, his rock-hard dick saluting her.

Seriously, the man had a body that would not quit.

Pressing her lips to his chest, she trailed her tongue down his stomach, reveling in the way his muscles tightened as she neared her prize. She dropped to her knees, taking his length in her hand and flicking her tongue across his tip.

He sucked in a sharp breath through his teeth and then moaned as she took him into her mouth as deeply as he'd go. Then she pulled back, gliding her tongue along the underside of his dick, circling it around the head before taking him in again.

His groans of pleasure thrilled her, and she couldn't remember a time making a man feel good was this enjoyable. She repeated the motions again and again, until his hands on her shoulders stilled her.

"You better come here, or this will be over before we even get started."

Releasing her hold, she rose to her feet. "We wouldn't want that, would we?"

"No, especially when I should be the one worshipping you." He cupped her breasts in his hands, teasing her nipples with his thumbs until they hardened into pearls. Then he bent down, taking one into his mouth, grazing her with his teeth as he unbuttoned her jeans and tried to work them over her hips.

Skinny jeans turned to shrink-wrap when they got wet, though, so hers weren't nearly as easy to remove. He smiled, though his brow furrowed as he pushed the fabric down. Her hips weren't having it. The pants would not budge.

"Here, let me help." Hooking her thumbs in the waistband, she wiggled her hips, working the denim down inch by inch. "Heck, if they'd had denim in the Middle Ages, they wouldn't have needed chastity belts. Give me a minute."

She shuffled deeper into the room, toward the bed, kicking off her flats on the way. At least her shoes weren't in cahoots with her traitorous pants.

As she got the fabric down around her knees, she tried one more heavy push, but all she managed was to lose her balance and fall backward onto the mattress.

Donovan chuckled and sauntered toward her. "I think I can take it from here."

He grabbed the fabric, peeling it down her legs and turning it inside out in the process. When he dropped the wet denim on the floor, she started to warn him about the smell, but thought better of it. She needed this man like she'd never needed anything in her life.

She scooted to the center of the bed, and he dove on top of her, covering her body with his, the warmth of his skin enveloping her like a blanket that was knitted solely for her.

He nipped her earlobe before trailing his lips down her neck, leaving a trail of fire in his wake. His teeth grazed her skin as he returned his attention to her breasts, teasing one with his fingers while sucking the other into his mouth and sending an electrical sensation tingling straight to her core.

She gasped as he released her, the cool air against her wet nipples hardening them even more as he continued his descent. He kissed his way down her stomach, gently pushing her legs apart until his shoulders fit between. Glancing down, she found him gazing at her, a longing in his eyes that took her breath away.

"Have I told you how beautiful you are?" His breath was warm against her skin.

"You're doing a pretty good job of showing me."

He chuckled, the sound a deep, melodious rumble from his chest. "You are intriguing." He kissed her right inner thigh. "Intelligent." He nipped at the left. "And irresistible." He blew a breath across her center.

"That's a lot of I's." She barely had any breath left in her lungs.

"I'm infatuated." He slipped out his tongue, bathing

her sensitive nub in moist heat, making her cry out with pleasure.

He moaned, the vibration of sound intensifying the sensation as he licked her, circling her clit until she arched her back, begging him for more. He slipped one finger inside her, and then a second, twisting his hand to reach her sweet spot and grazing it with the tips of his fingers over and over.

The orgasm coiled in her core, releasing like an explosion, consuming her from the inside out before putting her back together again. "Donovan, I need you," she panted.

He crawled on top of her, nuzzling into her neck. "Are you on birth control?"

"Yes." She tangled her fingers in his air. "And shifters are immune to disease."

With one swift thrust, he filled her, a pleasurable aching sensation expanding in her core as he pulled out and then filled her again. Rising onto his hands, he looked at her with hooded eyes as he rocked his hips, holding her gaze and making love to her with his entire being.

She wrapped her legs around his waist and clutched his biceps, matching his thrusts beat for beat until another climax consumed her. Clinging to him, she rode the wave of her orgasm, and he moaned, lowering his body to hers and wrapping his arms around her tightly as he pressed into her, finding his own release.

Her head spun for a moment, and as her breathing slowed, she traced her fingers along his sweat-slickened skin. She bit her lip, fighting her smile as he held her.

Donovan might not have been the answer to the town's prayers, but he *was* the answer to hers.

Alice was everything Donovan never knew he needed. As he lay on his back, with Alice snuggled into his side, he couldn't recall a time when he'd been more content. Now more than ever, he needed to unlock his magic so he could be the man she thought he was.

A sense of shame soured in his stomach. Though he'd never specifically said he had powers, the fact he had a familiar alluded to formidable magic. She undoubtedly assumed he was powerful, thanks to his masked aura. What a disappointment he would be when she learned otherwise.

She pressed her velvet-soft lips to his chest, drawing him from his thoughts, and then propped her head on her hand. "You're quiet. I hope it's because the sex was so good it left you speechless."

He smiled. "It was marvelous. So good, in fact, my legs have turned to rubber, and I'm afraid I won't be able to walk you to the door. Stay the night?"

"I can do that." She glided her fingers along his jaw. "But I have to be at the shop by ten."

"I'm not sure I'll be willing to let you go by then."

She arched a brow. "You'll have no choice. I'll fly away if you try to cage me."

"Noted." He ran his fingers through her silky black hair, tucking it behind her ear. "You're a free spirit. I would never try to hold you down."

"Good."

"Tell me more about Marcus Rainecourt's departure from this small slice of heaven. He never spoke of the town or the creek when he was alive."

Alice blew a breath through her nose, pursing her lips

as she shook her head. "He left before I was born, so everything I know is second-hand. He was not a well-liked man in this town."

"Nor was he in New York."

"He considered the shifters here second-class citizens, thought he was better than everyone else."

"That sounds about right." As she rested her hand on his chest, he covered it with his own.

"But he married a mundy. That's what we call humans here. Apparently, he thought having no magic at all was better than being a shifter... a small-town shifter, anyway. But his wife was from a small town too, so he had no right to look down his nose at us." She bristled as she spoke.

"You're passionate about equality."

"Well, yeah. People are people, no matter what kind of magic they have. It irks me to no end the way some think they're better than others just because their animal is a predator or they can cast spells and we can't or whatever."

She shook her head. "Anyway... Marcus's wife developed cancer. He took her to the creek to try and save her, but, of course, it did nothing to heal her since she was a mundy. The creek only heals those with magic in their blood."

"He never spoke of his wife either. Please, go on." How sad was it that Donovan was just now learning about his father's past? He'd made the mistake of asking about his former wife once as a child. The black eye he received in return ensured he never asked again.

"She died, and he was so distraught and angry at the creek, he packed up his kids and left. It wasn't the creek's fault, but..." She shrugged. "I mean, I get it. I've never lost anyone I loved, but I can imagine how heart-breaking it would be. He had a responsibility to this town, though, and now we're suffering right along with him."

"I am trying to get in touch with Griffin. He's most likely deep in the South American rainforest, and when he goes on one of his research missions, he leaves all technology behind. It will take time to get a message to him."

"Wouldn't it be easier to contact Matthias, then? We've gotten ahold of his assistant, but he refuses to return our calls."

"That's for the better. He would hurt more than he would help." Donovan was willing to suck it up when it came to Griffin. Matthias could fuck himself with a broomstick.

"Figures. Just like his old man." She bit her bottom lip. "That's not fair. I shouldn't cast judgment on people I've never met, but the animosity for that family runs deep in this town. Who knows? Maybe Marcus was a nice guy. Maybe he didn't know his exit would wreak havoc on the place where he grew up."

"Whether or not he knew the magic was tied to the family, I can't say. But I can assure you he was not a nice guy. Not in the slightest."

She laid her head on his shoulder, snuggling closer. "You're a nice guy."

"I try. And don't worry about Marty. He'll come around."

They lay there in silence for a few minutes, the length of her body pressed against him, warming him down to his soul. Her fingers grazed his skin, her delicate touch making his chest tighten with emotion. Where had she been all his life?

Right here in this town he should have known about. This town he was determined to save.

She traced a finger across his scar. "How did this happen?"

"I'd rather not say."

"It must have been caused by some wicked magic for the creek not to heal it."

He took her hand, bringing it to his mouth to kiss before holding it against the unmarred side of his chest. "It's nothing."

She yawned. "I hope you'll trust me enough to tell me the story someday."

The ache of guilt expanded in his chest. To tell her how he obtained the scar would be to admit he had no magic. His family had shamed him to the point he never admitted that detail to anyone.

And her disdain for his family—the entire town's disdain—would drive a wedge between them if he told her the truth.

Then again, she did say people were people no matter their magic. Surely she'd accept him as he was.

He rolled the idea over and over in his mind. The truth would be revealed eventually. She deserved to know it now.

With a deep inhale, he steeled himself for her reaction, whatever it might be. "Alice, there's something you should know about me."

She lay still, the gentle rise and fall of her chest the only movement she made.

"Alice?"

Her lips parted, and she snored softly on his shoulder.

CHAPTER ELEVEN

"How are you going to keep this place clean if you decide to live here? It's massive." Alice looked angelic wrapped in Donovan's midnight blue robe. She sat at the dinette in his breakfast room, sipping coffee, her hair still damp from her shower. He'd run her clothes through the wash this morning, and they should've been done in the dryer any minute.

"I suppose I'll hire a maid." He gazed into her emerald eyes, and his stomach fluttered.

She clutched her mug in both hands, inhaling the aroma of the coffee. "And a butler?"

"Why on earth would I need a butler?"

"I don't know. To answer the door? Help you get dressed?"

He laughed. "I'm quite capable of dressing myself."

"That's true. Though I hope you'll leave the *un*dressing to me." She grinned. "I'm quite capable of getting you naked."

"You certainly are." Not only was she good at getting him naked, she excelled at keeping him that way. They'd made love twice again this morning before reluctantly getting out of bed. He'd have preferred to spend the entire day naked with Alice, but he had work to do. He still hadn't found an artifact the warlock would accept in trade for the trowel, and no amount of money would change the man's mind.

She set her mug on the table and sashayed toward him, sinking into his lap and wrapping her arms around his shoulders. "I had a wonderful time last night."

He slid his hands up and down her back. "As did I."

She kissed him softly, brushing her tongue to his before nipping his bottom lip between her teeth. "I hope we can do it again soon. And again." She kissed his cheek. "And again."

Heat expanded in his chest, warming him down to his toes. "We do have a date planned for this evening."

"Heck yeah, we do." She bit her bottom lip, a question forming in her eyes. "Do you think it's too early to call Griffin? I have a committee meeting later this morning, and I'd love to have some good news for them."

Glancing at the clock, he nodded. "It's after eight. His assistant will be at the office."

"Would you mind?"

He could swallow his pride. For Alice, he could do anything. "I believe your clothes are dry. Why don't you go get dressed, and I'll see what I can do?"

Her smile brightened her eyes, melting his heart. "Thank you." She pressed a kiss to his cheek before sliding from his lap and padding toward the laundry room.

Donovan retrieved his phone from the bedroom and settled into a cigar chair in the study before opening his contacts and scrolling through to his brother's office.

Marty scurried into the room and perched on the arm of the chair. "Are you really going to do this?"

"I have no choice. Alice needs my assistance."

"Think about it first, boss. You're going to admit to your brother that you need magical help."

He paused, his thumb hovering above the call button. "It's Griffin. He'll be discreet." Griffin was the only one who treated Donovan with an ounce of respect.

"Really? You trust him not to mention it to Matthias? Because Matthias would poison the creek to spite you if he found out about this place."

Did he trust Griffin? Absolutely not. Donovan didn't trust anyone; he'd been burned too many times. He rubbed the scar on his chest. "Griffin hasn't spoken to Matthias in ten years. It will be fine."

Marty nodded. "Sure it will. You oughta tell Alice who you are and that you don't have any powers while you're at it. I mean, if you're going to destroy your reputation, you might as well go all in."

Donovan clenched his teeth. "I *will* tell her everything when the time is right."

He dialed the number, and Karen, Griffin's assistant, answered the phone.

"Good morning, Karen, it's Donovan Drake."

"Hello, Mr. Drake. How can I help you?" A lower-level witch with one human parent, Karen had always been kind to him.

"I need to get in touch with Griffin. It's a matter of utmost importance."

"He's on a charity mission in South America at the moment. I can take a message and pass it along the next time he checks in."

Donovan sighed. "Can you send a messenger? It's a life or death situation."

When his brother escaped on these humanitarian missions, he assimilated into the culture of the tribe he was helping, leaving his phone and any way to contact him behind.

"I'm sorry. I don't know his location."

"Please tell him to call me the moment you hear from him. I cannot express how important this matter is."

The clicking of a keyboard sounded through the receiver. "It will be the first message I relay."

"And, Karen, it's a delicate matter. Matthias is not to know of my request."

"Understood."

Alice padded into the room and sank onto the arm of the chair opposite from Marty as Donovan hung up the phone. "Any luck?"

"He's inaccessible, but his assistant will give him the message the next time he checks in."

Her shoulders slumped, the disappointment in her eyes tearing at his heart. "That's a bummer. I was hoping you'd be our ringer."

He rested a hand on her thigh. "All isn't lost yet. He'll return my call."

"Hopefully before it's too late." She stroked her fingers down Marty's side, and he swatted her hand away.

"Don't touch me. I'm a familiar, not a pet." He climbed onto Donovan's shoulder.

Alice held up her hands. "Donovan pets you all the time."

"That's because he's *my* warlock. Mine."

"Martin…" He took the mongoose from his shoulder and set him on the floor. "We'll have none of that."

Marty huffed and darted out of the room.

"I'm sorry about that." He tugged Alice into his lap.

She waved off his apology. "I should have asked his permission first."

"If it's any consolation, you can pet me anytime you want. No request for permission needed."

"Good to know." She cupped his cheek in her hand, running her thumb across his skin. "Not many shifters get to say they've met a super-powerful warlock like yourself, much less that they have permission to pet him."

A lump formed in his throat at her description of him. She couldn't have been more wrong.

"Speaking of your powers…" She batted her lashes. "We've had several different witches and warlocks cast spells on the creek, trying to fix the problem, but none were powerful enough to have a familiar."

"Really? I didn't realize we were so rare." Not that *we* was the best pronoun for him to use.

"In this part of the world, you are. Would you mind walking down to the creek with me this morning and giving it a try? I know you're not a Rainecourt, so it probably won't make a lick of difference, but we've exhausted all our other options."

"You mentioned the others all confirmed the necessity of a Rainecourt casting the spell. I should be no different."

"It's worth a try." She pleaded with her eyes, and his heart tore in two.

If he refused, she'd believe he didn't care. If he told her the truth, that he was a worthless stain on his family name, he wouldn't be able to look her in the eyes.

"Yeah, boss," Marty called from the doorway and snickered, "it's worth a try, isn't it?"

Donovan narrowed his gaze at his familiar before forcing a smile at Alice. "I will do my best."

They walked hand in hand to the creek, Alice chatting away about all the spells the other witches and warlocks had tried. Donovan had studied spellcasting extensively as a child. Even when it became obvious he'd never have the ability to cast his own, his father forced him to practice with his brothers, congratulating Matthias and Griffin for their successes while reminding Donovan what a disappointment he was.

What little Alice knew of the spells that were tried made them sound like basic witchcraft 101. Things he'd mastered—or would have mastered if he'd had an ounce of magic in his body—by the time he'd turned sixteen.

"Did no one attempt a healing ritual?" He kneeled on the bank, gazing at the water, unable to look at her.

"It's possible. I don't know much about casting spells or any kind of magic that doesn't involve shifting or…"

"Or?" He dared a glance at her, and she wrapped her arms around her middle, giving her head a small shake. "I will attempt healing magic. I sense that's what was used to bless the creek to begin with."

That wasn't a lie. He fully intended to attempt the incantation. The fact he already knew it wouldn't work because he'd never successfully cast a spell in his life was superfluous.

"What should I do?" She kneeled next to him, grinning, excitement rolling off her in waves.

"If you wouldn't mind, could you give me some space?"

"Right. Sorry." She scooted a few feet away. "This is thrilling. I've never seen you use your magic before."

He nodded and hovered his hands above the water,

whispering a healing incantation and calling on the spirits of the earth and stream to assist him.

He focused every fiber of his being into the spell. Never in his life had he wanted his magic to work more than this moment. His stomach bubbled, a burning sensation rolling upward to his chest, making his heart sprint.

Something was happening. Was the sensation his magic finally breaking free? Could it be that he simply needed Alice by his side to find a reason to *need* his magic?

The bubble of heat slid upward, burning the back of his throat. This was it! His magic was finally free!

He burped.

"Excuse me." Donovan closed his eyes. How incompetent could he be that he couldn't tell the difference between magic and gas?

Alice giggled. "Huevos rancheros can do that to you, especially when you're not used to salsa."

He rested his hands in his lap. "I'm so sorry. I'm afraid there's nothing I can do."

"Gotta be a Rainecourt?"

"Precisely."

She sighed and rose to her feet, dusting off her knees. "Thanks for trying. It means a lot."

They returned to the manor and stood in the foyer, face to face. How he managed to look her in the eyes now, he wasn't sure. He needed to tell her the truth. It wasn't fair to lead her on, letting her think he was a powerful warlock when he was no better than a human.

"I better get going," she said. "I've got a commissioned piece that's due today, and it's not going to finish itself."

"Shall I drive you?"

"I'll fly. It'll be good to stretch my wings." She reached

her arms out to her sides before placing her hands on his chest. "I had a wonderful time."

"Alice, I—" Before he could finish the thought, Marty climbed up his clothes and let loose a cloud of funk on his shoulder. The smell of Brussels sprouts and vinegar filled the foyer, and Alice covered her nose.

"Next time we order breakfast, we should go for bagels." She laughed and fanned the air in front of her face before kissing Donovan on the cheek. "I'll see you tonight."

He opened the door and watched in awe as she stepped onto the front porch, her body shimmering in emerald light as she transformed into a beautiful crow. She cawed, taking to the air, and Donovan returned inside.

"Impeccable timing, as always, Martin."

The familiar tilted his head. "What did I do?"

Donovan sighed.

"What's wrong?"

"I lied to her. Letting her assume I had powers was one thing, but now I've taken it too far."

Now, he wasn't just a failure; he was also a fraud. He was in it so deep, there was no way to dig himself out.

CHAPTER TWELVE

"Pull over and park by that tree." Excitement fizzed in Alice's blood as she pointed through the windshield. "It's a ten-minute walk to the springs from here."

Donovan killed the engine. "How long as the crow flies?"

She laughed. "Forty-five seconds tops, but I bet a warlock could cast a teleportation spell and be there instantly."

He slid out of the driver's seat and took a picnic basket from the back. "Given the choice to walk ten minutes by your side, I'll choose to hoof it every time."

She grinned and got out of the car. "Good choice."

"I've learned to enjoy the little things in life." He took her hand, and they walked side by side through the tall grass toward the source of the creek.

Though she hadn't seen Donovan *every* day over the past week and a half since their first date—a girl had to have some boundaries—the time she'd spent with him had been magical. He'd taken her to a couple of nice restaurants, and they'd even gone dancing one night, but the quiet time they spent alone was always her favorite.

When he'd suggested the idea of a picnic, she knew the perfect spot. A bluebonnet field surrounded the springs that sourced the creek, the dark blue flowers carpeting the green hills and filling the breeze with sweet perfume. Puffy white clouds dotted the sky, and the sun cast a blanket of warmth over the scene, making the setting absolutely pristine.

Light glinted on the surface of the water, shining like treasure, and her crow responded to the sight, happiness bubbling in her chest for both the location and the man next to her.

"A few more weeks, and it'll be too hot for a picnic in the middle of the day." She unfolded the blanket he'd handed her, laying it near the edge of the stream. "It gets sweltering by June."

"I can imagine." He sat on the blanket and unpacked the basket. Summer sausage, crackers, assorted cheeses, grapes, and a bottle of wine made up the spread he'd planned. "It's warm already."

She laughed. "Just wait 'til August... If you're still here, that is." Gods, she hoped he'd still be here. She couldn't get enough of this man.

He popped the cork and filled two plastic cups with red wine before handing one to her. Sidling next to her, he clinked their glasses together and took a sip. "Every day I spend with you makes the idea of staying here permanently more and more appealing."

"Hmm..." She leaned into him, pressing a kiss to his lips. "You know I'm a sure thing at this point, so you don't have to tease me like that to get into my pants."

He nuzzled her neck, and the feel of his warm breath

on her ear raised goosebumps on her skin. "I would never tease you, Alice. I mean every word of that."

"Hot diggity dog."

"Indeed." He kissed her again, and the taste of pinot noir on his lips made her head spin in a delightful way.

Alice's crow cawed her approval in her mind. This man could be the one. How else could she explain the hard and fast way she was falling head over tail feathers for him? Her rational side warned her she should probably put on the brakes. Not a screeching halt, but a slight slowdown would have been wise.

But Alice had never been accused of doing the wise thing. She wasn't an owl, for Pete's sake. She much preferred to live in the moment, and this moment couldn't have been any better.

After they ate, she lay on her back, resting her head in Donovan's lap. He smiled down at her, running his fingers through her hair, and she basked in the attention. "It's a shame Marty didn't want to come. I thought he'd enjoy the outdoors."

Donovan sighed. "Normally, he would. I've never shown so much interest in a woman before, so it's hard for him to get used to this. He'll come around, though. You make me happy, and he'll learn to accept that."

"You make me happy too." Her lids drifted shut as he continued stroking her hair. "My parents used to bring me here for picnics when I was a kid. The creek was a lot deeper then, and Megan and I would swim all day while our parents sat on the bank and talked."

"You two are close."

"We're like sisters. Well, I'm an only child, so I assume it's what having a sibling would be like." She opened her eyes. "What about you? What's your family like? You don't mention them much."

"There's not much to say. We were never close, and now I'm alone." He stared out over the water. "How many generations of your family have lived here?"

"Just us. My parents visited Shift Creek when they first got married, and they fell in love with the town. So, they moved here and opened the café a few years before I was born."

"Have you ever considered moving away?"

"Heck no." She sat up. "I went to college in Austin, and that was enough. I'm a free spirit, but I'm not a wanderer. I'll take a vacation every now and then, but Shift Creek is my home. I love it here. Why?"

Her stomach sank. If this was the part where he asked her to move to New York with him, he would be sorely disappointed. Best to find out now if he was having second thoughts about staying. "Do you want to go back to New York? Is that why you asked?"

"No. I've never had such an affinity for a place like you do. Anywhere could be my home."

He always had the right answer for everything, didn't he?

As she stretched her arms over her head, a gust of wind picked up an empty wine cup, blowing it through the field. "I'll get it." Alice stood and chased the tumbling plastic a few yards before grabbing it and returning it to the picnic basket.

Donovan's phone lay in the bottom of the bin next to his keys and wallet, and a notification lit up his screen. He stood on the creek bank, watching the springs bubble from underground.

"You have a message." She gestured to the basket and tried not to get her hopes up.

"I'm sure it can wait." He reached a hand toward her, inviting her to join him.

"What if it's Griffin?"

He nodded once and strode to the basket, lifting the phone and swiping his thumb across the screen. His eyes darkened briefly before he dropped it on the blanket. "It's not."

"Damn." She followed him back to the water's edge and nudged him playfully with her hip. "Was it something important?"

He nudged her back and smiled. "Not at all. I'm attempting to acquire an artifact...for a client...but the current owner is reluctant to part with it."

"Can't you cast a spell to make him think he doesn't want it?" She wiggled her fingers toward him like a cartoon witch about to shoot magic from her hands. Why she did that, she had no clue. She'd seen witches and warlocks cast spells before, and they were never that animated. They weren't green and warty either.

Well, some of them were warty, but that had nothing to do with their magical abilities.

Donovan arched a brow. "That would be unethical... and illegal."

"Oh, yeah. I guess it would. What about love spells? Are those illegal? Because I could swear you slipped a potion into my tea to make me feel the way I do."

"How do you feel?" He reached for her hand, lacing their fingers together.

Her heart rate kicked up like it did every time he touched her, and she held his gaze as she searched for the right words to describe her emotions. "Like I hit the jackpot at a Lake Charles casino, and the coins are so shiny, my crow is beside herself with giddiness. Seriously, she won't stop cawing in my head."

He tucked a strand of hair behind her ear. "The feeling is mutual, and I promise it's not from a spell."

"What are you going to tell your client about the artifact?"

"Not to worry. My negotiation skills are unmatched."

"Ooo…" She walked her fingers up his arm. "Somebody thinks highly of himself."

He chuckled and looked at the creek. "How high did the water used to reach?"

"All the way up to our blanket twenty years ago." She gestured to their picnic a few yards away.

"How deep is it now?"

"Let's find out." She pushed him over the edge, which in hindsight wasn't the smartest thing she could have done. He was fifty pounds heavier and twenty times stronger than her, and when he latched on to her wrist, he almost dragged her into the water with him.

But Alice was quick, and she shifted like her life depended on it, her wing slipping from his grasp as she took to the sky, while he landed in the creek with a giant *kersploosh*.

He sputtered as he shot to his feet, wiping the water from his eyes. "Payback is a bitch, Alice," he called, laughing as she circled above. "Just wait."

She landed in the grass and shifted to human, smiling sheepishly. "Sorry about that. I couldn't help myself."

"I'm sure." He smiled and shook his head. "It's deeper here than on my property. It's nice." Peeling his shirt off, he threw it onto the bank before sinking deeper in the water and taking off his shoes.

He tossed those next to his shirt and swam toward the edge, looking at her with so much heat in his gaze, her clothes nearly melted off on their own. "It's a shame I'm swimming alone."

How did he do that with just his eyes? Honestly, the water covered him up to his neck, so it was simply the look on his face that had her hormones spinning into overdrive. "You're right. Swimming alone is dangerous." She took off her shirt and slipped out of her pants. "What if you got a cramp and needed to be rescued? I couldn't help you from the bank."

Biting her lip, she glanced around to be sure no one else had decided to trek out this far for a picnic and then shimmied out of her remaining clothes. She dropped them on the blanket, folding it over to cover the evidence, and then folded it one more time for good measure before jumping into the creek, naked as a jaybird.

Donovan took her in his arms, and she wrapped her legs around his waist. "Why do you think it's only jays who are referred to as naked?" she asked.

"Good question." He slid his hands across her bare back. "My crow captures the epitome of naked beauty. From now on, the expression will be 'naked as a crow.'"

Alice giggled, her stomach fluttering. "Oh, I'm *your* crow, am I?"

"I don't intend to share you."

"I don't want to be shared." *Hot damn.* Did he have any idea how sexy he was? She was about to show him.

Reaching for the button on his jeans, she glanced over his shoulder and found a game warden approaching through the brush. "Crap on a cracker!" She slid from Donovan's arms and sank below the surface up to her neck. "I can't afford another mark on my record."

"*Another* mark? What have you been arrested for?" He rose to his feet, standing between her and the officer's view.

"Just trespassing, but the judge said if he saw me again, next time I'd serve jail time." She could *not* go to jail. Not if she ever wanted a chance in city politics.

Donovan rested his hands on her shoulders. "It's not illegal to swim in the creek, is it?"

"No, but I'm naked! Skinny dipping on public land is most definitely illegal. Can't you freeze him for a minute or something? Give me time to put my clothes on?"

He pursed his lips. "Can you fly with wet feathers?"

"Yes, but—"

"Fly away. I'll handle the game warden."

"Are you sure?" She crossed her arms over her chest as if she could hide her nakedness. What was she thinking jumping into the creek in broad daylight wearing nothing but her birthday suit?

That she was going to get lucky. That was what.

"He's only human," Donovan whispered, "and I'm not doing anything wrong."

"I don't want you to take all the heat, but I seriously can't go to jail."

"I'm not naked, so there'll be no heat. Go." He glanced over his shoulder at the officer and gestured with his hands for her to leave.

"Thank you." She shifted, splashing with her wings in the creek until Donovan gave her a boost and she caught wind. She flapped hard, raining droplets across the surface of the water as she made her way to a nearby tree to land on a branch.

Donovan turned to the game warden as he approached and lifted a hand to wave. "Good afternoon, Officer."

From her spot in the tree, Alice could just make out the man's name tag, which read Carter.

Officer Carter stopped by their picnic, tracing his gaze over the folded blanket—thank goodness she'd hidden the evidence—before eyeing Donovan's wet shirt and shoes on the bank. "Where's the woman who was here?"

Donovan furrowed his brow. "There's no woman here. I'm alone."

Carter cast his gaze upstream and down before removing his sunglasses. "I heard a woman's voice."

"Perhaps it was the wind through the trees? I assure you I've been alone since I arrived."

"Hmph," Carter grunted. "You're having a picnic alone, all the way out here at the springs?"

Donovan lifted his hands. "What can I say? I heard it was a magical place, and I wanted to check it out for myself to see if it lives up to its reputation."

"Don't tell me you believe in that BS warlock story the townsfolk made up. It's a crock of horse manure." He tucked his glasses into his shirt pocket and rested his hands on his hips.

Donovan waded toward the shore. "Actually, I do. You see, I'm a warlock myself."

Holy heck! What did he think he was doing? Surely he had a plan and wasn't outing himself to this mundy. The supes of Shift Creek worked hard to keep their magic a secret.

"Oh yeah?" Carter laughed, unimpressed. "If you're a warlock, show me a magic trick."

Donovan glanced up at Alice in the tree, and she cawed, flapping her wings. She really wanted to yell, "Don't be crazy!" but in her crow form, she did the best she could.

"Sadly, I can't." He held her gaze, and she sighed with relief.

He returned his attention to the game warden. "I was born with my magic locked. I came to Shift Creek hoping the magical properties would heal my broken powers, and I could be the warlock I was always meant to be. Alas, my plan didn't work. I'm afraid your creek doesn't recognize my locked magic, and it's done nothing to fix my problem."

This time Carter's laugh was genuine. "Good one." He returned his sunglasses to his face. "Don't leave any trash behind. Littering is illegal."

"No worries, Officer. I won't mess with Texas." He looked up at Alice, and she expected a wink or a smile, but he kept in character until the game warden walked away. Then, he climbed out of the creek, slipped on his shoes, and gathered up Alice's clothes along with the picnic.

She flew ahead, landing on the roof of his Audi as the officer climbed into his SUV and drove away.

Donovan didn't say a word as he opened the passenger door and laid her clothes on the console before strolling around to the driver's side and getting in. Alice dove into the car and shifted to human, slamming the door and sliding down in the seat to wiggle into her clothes.

"That was classic." She laughed as she pulled her shirt over her head and brushed her hair out of her face. "The way you made up that story on the fly about being a warlock without powers was impressive. You seemed so sincere, I almost believed you."

He started the car and pulled onto the road. "What if it wasn't a story? What if it were true?"

She laughed again. "That would be something."

"Indeed it would."

She rested her hand on his thigh. "Thanks for saving my hide back there. I appreciate it."

He shrugged. "It was nothing."

"No, I mean it." She cupped his cheek in her hand, gliding her thumb along his skin. "You lied for me, and you didn't have to do that. It means a lot."

He took her hand and kissed her palm. "It was the least I could do."

CHAPTER THIRTEEN

"I'm sorry, Donovan, he hasn't checked in yet." Karen's voice was kind and cheerful as usual.

He'd contacted his brother's assistant two weeks ago, after his first night with Alice, but she'd had no news of Griffin's location then either.

"Does he usually go this long between check-ins?" He ground his teeth, frustration gnawing in his gut. They'd endured several days of thunderstorms over the week, which helped the level of the creek to rise a bit, but the rain had done nothing to restore the waning magic.

"He's gone months before. I wouldn't worry about him. He leaves a crystal that's tied to his life energy, so if he's ever in trouble, it will glow red. It's been a cool blue since he left."

"I'm not concerned about his safety, Karen." He clamped his mouth shut. That had sounded much harsher than he intended. "Apologies. I don't mean to take my frustration out on you, but this town is in crisis, and only Griffin can save it."

"I'll relay the message the moment he checks in."

"Thank you. Have a pleasant rest of your day." He pressed "end" and leaned his head back on the sofa, pinching the bridge of his nose as he squeezed his eyes shut. He'd scoured all his sources for magical artifacts—even the dark web—and he was prepared to pay any price for a relic that might save the creek.

Sadly, such an artifact didn't exist. To make matters worse, the warlock he'd been in discussions with over the enchanted trowel pulled out of the negotiations before they could reach an agreement, erasing his digital footprint and virtually disappearing.

Not that Donovan could have stolen the creek's magic anyway. To drain it now, when it couldn't regenerate itself, would be detrimental. Even if he did manage to unlock his own powers, he couldn't replicate a two-hundred-year-old spell when he had no idea how or why it had been cast in the first place.

His brother needed to get here before the stream lost its magic completely. It was the only way to save the town. Donovan knew now that Alice would never leave this place. It was her home, and he wanted it to be his as well.

"Still no luck finding Griffin?" Marty climbed up his pantleg and perched in his lap.

"None." He straightened his spine and stroked his familiar's wiry fur. Moonlight streamed in through the floor-to-ceiling windows in the back of the house, giving the tree line in the distance a silvery glow.

"I say we cut our losses and head back home. That creek's not gonna help you, and once it dries up, they'll crucify you when they find out who you are."

Donovan closed his eyes again. He'd been fully prepared to tell Alice everything the first time she spent the night with him. Then she'd fallen asleep, and he hadn't mustered the courage again since he faked the spell on the creek. She'd found his truth so humorous when he confessed to the game warden on their picnic, he hadn't found a moment that felt right to tear their relationship apart with honesty.

Not only was he a fraud, he was a coward. He could admit as much.

"I'm going to tell her everything tomorrow." He had to. "If she accepts me, you'll have to get used to this place. It will be our home."

Marty narrowed his eyes and hopped off Donovan's lap, scurrying to the opposite end of the couch. "If we hadn't lost that amulet, you'd have taken the creek's magic, and we'd be home in New York by now."

"You're right, we would, but I'm glad we lost it. Fate brought us here, my friend. Alice and I are meant to be."

"That's your man-bits talking."

Donovan arched a brow. "Excuse me?"

"I don't trust her, boss. She's hiding something."

"Martin…" He scooped the familiar into his arms. "If you would give her a chance, I'm sure she would grow on you."

"Like a fungus." He wiggled free and returned to the other end of the sofa. "She's trying to take you away from me."

"She's not…" He blew out a frustrated breath. "I'm here with you tonight, aren't I? When I told her you and I needed some bonding time, she took no issue with it. Why do you take issue when I bond with her?"

Marty sat upright and crossed his tiny arms over his chest. "I told you, I don't trust her. You shouldn't either."

"I promise to be careful. That will have to do." Though

how careful he could be when the woman already held his heart in her beak, he had no clue.

"Fine." Marty hopped to the floor, letting one rip on his way down. "Let's get a pizza. I'm starving."

The scent of day-old bacon fat mixed with garbage wafted to Donovan's senses. "Perhaps something with a little less grease. I'm not sure I can endure the night if you have a stomachache."

Alice scrambled out of the dumpster, dragging a dented pie plate behind her. Raccoon paws were super handy when it came to collecting pieces for their art. No wonder Megan always had a better haul when they did this.

A caw echoed through the alley, and she looked up to see Megan as her crow swooping down and dropping a bedazzled hair clip before landing gracefully beside her. Alice picked it up and examined the piece. The clasping mechanism didn't work, which was probably why the owner had tossed it, but the green and blue stones encrusting it would make a great addition to her ocean mural. She nodded her approval before dropping it in the pile they'd made.

Megan hopped to the end of the alley and glanced both ways down the cross street. She nodded and flapped Alice's wings twice, the all-clear signal, before flying back toward her. It was so weird seeing someone else in her crow form, but the animal part of her didn't seem to mind. Her human side, however, got antsy when they were separated, so the power swap never lasted long.

Alice shifted to human form and took back her crow,

returning Megan's borrowed raccoon. "You're getting good at those landings."

"Thanks. Ooh, nice haul. You're getting good with my paws." She scooped half the items into her arms. "Let's get these back to the shop and clean them up."

Alice picked up the rest of the soon-to-be art pieces and followed her into the town square.

They'd swapped animals several times over the past few weeks. A fresh set of eyes in their usual hotspots had yielded quite the finds. Alice was used to searching from the sky, so she could overlook things that Megan caught as her crow, and the same was true when she went dumpster diving as a raccoon.

"I thought you were supposed to spend the night with Donovan." Megan unlocked the shop door and held it open for Alice. "Did you hit a pothole on Lover's Lane?"

"More like a speedbump...in the form of a talking mongoose." She stepped inside, and Megan followed.

"Farty Marty still doesn't like you?"

"He's got jealousy issues. Donovan thought some bonding time between the two of them might help." Alice paced to the backroom and set her treasures on the table. "I imagine the little guy feels like a child when his single dad brings home a potential new mommy."

"You'll win him over. Everyone likes you."

"Everyone but Farty Marty."

Megan soaked a chipped candle holder with disinfectant and scrubbed the surface with a sponge. "Seriously, though, everyone in this town likes you. Have you ever considered running for city council? Or, hell, you'd make a great mayor!"

"The thought has crossed my mind. We could use another supe at city hall." She sighed. "The mundies found a company to dredge the creek, and since there are more of them in office, they voted to approve it."

"Oh, no." Megan dropped the sponge. "They can't mess with elemental magic. They'll destroy it."

"The supes on council convinced them to give it one more full moon, but even with Donovan's help, we haven't been able to contact the Rainecourts. Christine is flying out to New York this week to try and force her way into Matthias's office. Griffin is still MIA."

Megan toyed with the candle holder, turning it over in her hands as her mouth screwed up to the side—her thinking face. "What if we faked it? Just for now to give us some more time."

Alice polished a tarnished soup ladle and set it on the table. "What do you mean?"

"Maybe Donovan can cast a spell on the full moon to fake the shift in flow. The mundies will think all is well, and we'll have another month to get a Rainecourt out here to fix it for real. Preferably Griffin." She winked.

"That would take some major magic." She shook her head. "I don't know if he could do it. Aside from the healing spell he tried to cast on the creek, I've never seen him use his powers." She laughed. "Did I tell you we attempted skinny dipping at the springs?"

Megan's mouth dropped open. "What? No, you did not!"

"We did. Well…I did. Donovan still had his pants on when the mundy game warden showed up, but I was buck naked."

"Nice!" Megan laughed.

"I shifted and flew away, and Donovan talked his way out of trouble. He made up some story about how he was a warlock born without magic. The officer got a good laugh out of it. So did I. Can you imagine?"

"What if it were true?"

"As if." She paused, chewing her lip. "If it were, I hope he'd tell me. He ought to trust me by now. But he's got a familiar, so it's obviously not."

"Yeah, and look at his aura," Megan said. "It practically crackles with power."

"He's got more magic than a stray dog has fleas."

Megan picked up a rusted spade and sprayed it with disinfectant. "The fact that he doesn't use his gift much is more proof of his power. The really strong ones are like that. When they've got nothing to prove, they don't flaunt their magic. You don't go around showing everyone your crow, right? It's always been part of you, so it's no big deal."

Alice smiled. That was one of the things she loved about Donovan. His wealth and power hadn't corrupted him in the slightest. He was guarded, sure, and he had his secrets. But who didn't? She enjoyed unraveling the mystery of Donovan Drake.

"Faking the creek's flow is a good idea, actually. I'll talk to him about it tomorrow." She finished cleaning the pieces and washed her hands. "I'm heading up to bed. I haven't had a lot of sleep the past couple of weeks, so I'm going to take advantage tonight."

Megan grinned. "I bet. I'll lock up on my way out. See you tomorrow."

Alice climbed the stairs to her apartment and padded into the bedroom. As she hung the amulet on her jewelry tree, a pang of guilt flashed in her chest. She needed to tell Donovan about the amulet. Either that or throw it out for real. Things were going so well between them; the last thing she needed was to splash turpentine on the beautiful painting of their relationship.

But it was so much fun to swap magic with Megan...

She would tell him. He knew she was a salvage artist, and it was no secret how she and Megan found their supplies. There was no reason to be embarrassed anymore. Yes, Donovan was sophisticated, wealthy...even proper. But he was also kind, patient, and accepting. He would understand.

After a quick shower, Alice cracked a window to let in the cool spring breeze and climbed into bed, snuggling under her fluffy yellow duvet. She'd grown accustomed to falling asleep next to Donovan's scrumptiously warm body, and she ached to feel his strong arms wrapped around her.

The pillow she clutched to her chest was a sorry replacement, but it would have to do. She closed her eyes, her lips curving into a smile as she recalled their most recent romp between the sheets. The man knew how to keep a girl satisfied, that was for sure. And wanting more. And more, and more. She couldn't get enough of her sexy warlock.

Before she could make the descent into sleep, something thudded on the floor near the window. She froze, slowly opening her eyes and half-expecting to find a burglar or a murderer—or both—standing above her with a knife.

But she was on the second floor for goodness' sake. It wasn't like someone would scale the side of the building to slip in through the cracked window. Unless they were an animal...

"Who's there?" She sat upright, squinting against the darkness, but she couldn't see the culprit.

Claws skittered on the hardwood, and a drawer slid

open before thudding shut.

"Megan? Is that you?" Alice scrambled out of bed and flipped on a light. "Marty?!"

Donovan's familiar sat atop her dresser, his beady eyes widening as he gasped. "Crap." He snatched a handful of necklaces from her jewelry tree and darted toward the window.

Alice had fast reflexes, though—thanks to her animal side—and she grabbed him around his little body, necklaces scattering across the floor as she lifted him in front of her. "You little thief!"

"I'm not the thief."

Alice closed her window and dropped Marty into an antique birdcage, latching the door shut. Yes, it might have been weird for a crow to keep a birdcage in her bedroom, but it wasn't like she locked any birds in it. The piece was beautiful, made of dark metal with an intricate cast-iron crow sitting on the loop where it attached to the stand. She appreciated the irony of the bird being on top of the cage rather than in it.

Snatching her phone from the bedside table, she dialed Donovan's number.

"Hello?" His voice was raspy with sleep, and if she wasn't so perturbed with his klepto-familiar, she might have enjoyed the sexy little shiver running down her spine.

"You need to come get your mongoose," she snapped.

"What?" The sound of sheets rustled through the line. "Marty is there? I put him to bed two hours ago."

"Well, he didn't stay. I caught him trying to steal my jewelry. Taking things others have discarded as trash is one thing, but I draw the line at breaking and entering." She inhaled a deep breath, trying to rein in her frustration. It wasn't Donovan's fault his familiar was a thief.

"I'll be right over."

She tossed her phone on the nightstand and plopped onto the edge of the bed, crossing her arms and tapping her foot as she glared at Marty. "What were you trying to accomplish by stealing my stuff?"

He crossed his stubby arms and glared in return.

"If you're trying to drive me away, it won't work. I care about him, and I'm not going to let a thieving mongoose come between us."

Marty gawked. "*Me* come between *you*? *You're* the one who's splitting us up. Homewrecker!"

"Homewrecker?! How dare—" She ground her teeth. Arguing with a talking animal was not a productive way to spend her time. If she wanted to be with Donovan, she'd have to win over Marty. Warlocks and their familiars had unbreakable bonds.

"Listen, I think we got off on the wrong foot. The whole ordeal with me giving him my crow and putting you in the jar… I wasn't trying to hurt either of you. I wasn't even sure how it happened. I'm not trying to divide you and Donovan. I want to be your friend."

"Hmph." The little rat turned his back to her. *The nerve!*

Twenty minutes later, Donovan knocked on her door. She left Marty in the cage to answer, and Donovan stepped in wearing sweatpants and a dark gray t-shirt. His hair was disheveled from sleep, and she fought the urge to drag him into the kitchen and make a meal out of him before they addressed the situation.

"I'm so sorry." He kissed her on the cheek. "I don't know what's gotten into him. He's never done this before."

"He hates me. Plain and simple." She led him up the stairs.

"He doesn't hate you." He followed her to the bedroom and stopped in the doorway, shaking his head. "Martin, what have you done?"

"Reconnaissance. I told you not to trust her." He rose onto his haunches and gripped the bars of the cage like a tiny furry prisoner.

Donovan blew out a heavy breath. "I'm so very sorry, Alice. I will have words with him when we get home." He unlatched the door, and Marty climbed up his arm to sit on his shoulder.

"She's a thief, boss. Look down there." He gestured toward the dresser, where the amulet lay half-hidden beneath it.

Doo-doo on a donut. This was not how she wanted Donovan to find out about it. Her heart sank into her stomach, and her hands involuntarily clenched into fists. Her fight-or-flight instinct flipped all the way to flight, her crow begging to take over and fly her the heck away from the awkwardness that was about to ensue.

"Where did you get this?" Donovan kneeled and picked up the amulet by the chain, cradling the stone in his hand as if it were precious.

Alice's jaw worked, but she couldn't form words.

"She stole it from you," Marty sneered. "The first night we arrived, remember? The crow on the balcony really was her!"

Donovan looked at her with disbelief. "Alice, is this true?"

"What? No, of course not!" She crossed her arms and let out a sardonic laugh. "I mean…" *Oh, damn it all to hell. Yes, H-E-L-L. This is too messed up for heck. I saved that little weasel's life, and this is how he repays me?*

She chewed her bottom lip as Donovan held her gaze, and Marty's beady little eyes bore into her like hot pokers.

"Alice?" Donovan's brow furrowed.

"Yes, okay? I was the crow on your balcony that night, but I did not steal the amulet. I found it in the trash outside the house."

"Listen to her, boss. She can't even come up with a decent excuse. Like you'd ever put a priceless artifact in the garbage."

He closed his fist around the pendant, his eyes tightening with mistrust. "How much did you hear that night?"

The accusation in his voice ruffled her feathers. Aside from eavesdropping—and lying about being there—she'd done absolutely nothing wrong. "Not much. You were looking for something you'd lost. That's all."

"And you didn't consider the thing I'd lost might have been this?" He held up the amulet.

"It was *in the trash*. I literally took it from the garbage can that had been set out on the side of the road for the trash collectors to pick up and take to the dump."

"Don't believe her," Marty said. "She must've snuck in when we weren't looking and taken it right from the satchel."

Donovan's nostrils flared. "You were wearing this the first time I came into your shop, weren't you? This is how you turned me into a bird."

"Yes." She crossed her arms. "Donovan, you have to believe me. I'm sorry I lied about being at your house, but I would never steal. I only ever take things that people have discarded. Since it was in the trash, I thought you didn't want it."

He shook his head. "You've had it all this time. You've

been hiding it from me."

All right, that she could admit to. She had been hiding it, but who could blame her? "I was embarrassed, okay? I got it out of your garbage, and I didn't want you to judge me for dumpster diving."

"I know how you get your art supplies, Alice." His voice was sharp, his teeth clenched.

"I know. And I'm not embarrassed anymore. I was going to tell you about it tomorrow. I thought we'd have a good laugh about how silly it is to hide things from each other, and everything would be okay."

He inhaled deeply, his head shaking as he lifted his arms and dropped them at his sides. "Everything is not okay. You deceived me."

"I didn't."

"You did." He moved toward the door.

"Donovan, wait." She reached for him, but he turned and headed down the stairs.

"I won't discuss this now." He opened the front door.

She stopped halfway down the steps. "If not now, when?"

He paused and turned to her, the pain in his eyes palpable. "I don't know."

"Later, gator." Marty snickered as Donovan closed the door behind him.

Alice stood there, her mouth hanging open as a car door slammed and the engine purred to life. Did he just...? What the...?

"Freaking farting mongoose!" The man she loved just called her a liar and thief. How could he possibly accuse her of stealing after everything they'd shared?

Wait... The man she...?

Fan-friggin-tastic. She was in love with Donovan.

CHAPTER FOURTEEN

"I can't believe she had the amulet the entire time." Donovan's heart was breaking as he strode down to the creek with Marty perched on his shoulder. Three days had passed since he'd learned the truth about Alice, but he still couldn't wrap his mind around it. "Even you were certain she didn't have it."

"I was wrong, but we caught the crow red-beaked, boss. Believe it."

He couldn't. He didn't want to. "Why, Marty? Why would she steal it from me?" A hollow ache expanded in his chest, threatening to swallow him whole. "I trusted her." And trust wasn't something he gave easily.

He'd spent his entire life watching his back, trying in vain to prove his worth, to show his father he was worthy of the Rainecourt legacy. But the legacy had been a lie.

This town, this creek was his legacy, yet he'd come with the intent of taking magic his family was meant to nurture. Lifting the amulet with a trembling hand, he watched it glint in the sunlight. In his effort to prove himself to a dead man, he'd turned out just like his father. Self-serving and insolent.

Donovan was no better than a common thief. Who was he to judge Alice?

"You're better off without her," Marty said.

He kneeled on the edge of the bank. "I love her."

"You do?" Marty jumped to the ground beside him.

"I thought I did." He squeezed his eyes shut and sat back on his heels. "I do. It simply doesn't make sense for her to steal it and then lie about the theft when she had it in her possession."

"Those crows can be tricky. Don't forget she crapped on my head too."

His lips twitched. "If I recall, you were trying to have her for dinner."

"So?"

"Perhaps the bomb was well-deserved." He smiled sadly. Dull moments didn't exist when Alice was around.

"C'mon, boss. You've waited long enough. Use the amulet to take the magic, and let's get the hell out of this place. I haven't had a decent slice of pizza since we got here."

Donovan gazed at the shallow water, the level now at least a foot lower than when Alice had found him here weeks ago.

Alice. She loved this town and everyone in it. Without the magic of the creek, they'd lose their tourism. Her art studio wouldn't survive, nor would the coffee shop or the café. Megan had informed him how dire the situation was when she showed up on his doorstep two days ago, begging him to cast a spell to temporarily reverse the flow of the creek to buy them more time.

Of course, he'd denied her request, his excuse as flimsy

as single-ply toilet paper. A cloaking spell would have done the trick, but he'd told her only an elemental warlock could accomplish the feat.

And so the lies continued, while the creek ailed.

Perhaps Marty was right. Perhaps they should cut their losses and leave town. Gods knew Alice would be better off without him. She deserved so much more than he'd given her.

"How could I have been so foolish, Marty? I could never face her after what I've done, but I can't imagine my life without her." Pressure built in the back of his eyes as he tilted his head toward the sky.

Marty rested a paw on his leg. "She means that much to you?"

"I would gladly give up my pursuit of magic if I could have her by my side forever." Those were the most honest words to pass his lips since he arrived in this town.

"Oh, boss." Marty rubbed his paws down his furry face. "I feel terrible."

"As do I, my friend." He patted the familiar on the head.

"You know, maybe you could talk to her." He stared at the ground. "It's possible she did find the amulet in the trash."

"How? It was in the satchel with you. I had convinced myself I'd accidentally thrown it away, but I've never been that careless."

A low growling sound emanated from Marty's throat as he shrank inward. "It was in the garbage because... because I put it there." He covered his face with his paws.

"You...put it there?" Donovan blinked, his mind reeling. "Why, Martin?"

The mongoose sighed heavily. "Because I was afraid

once you got your magic, you wouldn't want me anymore. If you're as powerful as your brothers, you'll be able to find a real familiar, and you won't need me."

"You *are* a real familiar."

"Yeah, but I'm not *your* familiar. Not really. I don't want to be put up for sale again. Stuck in a cage until someone offers the right price. Starved. Beaten when I talk back." His lower jaw trembled. "I don't want to lose you."

Donovan sat in the grass next to him. "So Alice really did find the amulet in the trash." And he'd accused her of stealing. Add another mark against him. "And you went to her apartment to get it back? You knew she had it all this time?"

"I'm sorry, boss. I saw it on her the first time you met, and I lied about it. I thought you'd give up, and we'd go back home, but then you started seeing her, and..."

Donovan ground his teeth. In a way, he could understand Marty's actions. He knew first-hand what it felt like to not really belong. But to sabotage his chance at both getting his magic to work and at finding love...

"I'm speechless, Martin. I've never been more disappointed." In both the familiar and in himself. He was tired of living a lie.

"Do you want me to go? I can live in the forest with the mundane animals. Just please don't put me up for sale."

Donovan shook his head. "I don't want you to go. We've both made mistakes since we arrived in this town, and I believe it's time we righted our wrongs."

His stomach soured as he tugged his phone from his pocket and scanned the contacts for Matthias's number. He was loath to call his eldest brother. What was left of his pride reeled against the upcoming conversation, but what choice did he have? If he could restore the magic to the creek, perhaps Alice would forgive him. She was worth whatever insults Matthias would throw at him.

He swallowed the bile from his throat and pressed the call button.

"Well, well." Matthias sounded vilely amused as he always did when Donovan spoke to him. "If it isn't the little slug trying to slime his way into my good graces."

Donovan's skin crawled, but he refused to take the bait. "I hope you're well, Matthias."

"I'm a master warlock and head of the Rainecourt fortune. Of course I'm well." He laughed. "If you're calling to ask for money, Father made it clear in his will the run-down shack in Texas was all you were to receive."

"I don't need your money. I've made plenty on my own, and that 'shack'…" He ground his teeth. If his brother thought the manor was nothing more than a hovel, it was best to let him continue with that belief. "There's a magical creek that runs through the town, and its power is deteriorating."

"Don't tell me you actually believe in that little marketing ploy."

Donovan picked up Marty and headed toward the house. "It's not a ploy. A Rainecourt ancestor blessed the spirit of the creek, and only a warlock from our bloodline can help."

"Why don't you do it, then? Oh, right… Because you're not a real warlock."

"Please, Matthias." It pained him to grovel, especially to a narcissistic dickhead, but this was for Alice.

"I'm a busy man, D. Small town gimmicks don't concern me, and you'd be better off not getting involved. Father abandoned that place for a reason."

"If you would just—"

"I'm busy." The line went dead.

Donovan stepped into the foyer and closed the door, gripping the knob so tightly the damn thing nearly came off in his hand. "That went as well as expected."

"I don't know why you bothered with him. Did you forget about the time he turned me into a cockroach just to be an ass? We're lucky Griffin took pity and changed me back, or I'd still be an insect."

Donovan scratched beneath his chin. "At least you'd be pocket-sized."

"Not funny, boss." He scrambled down the front of Donovan's shirt and hopped to the floor. "What's the plan now?"

"For the creek, I don't know. For Alice, there's only one thing I can do."

"You're seriously done with him?" Megan emptied the cash register and carried the money to the safe.

Alice leaned in the doorway, trying to ignore the nausea that had been churning in her stomach since the night Donovan found out about the amulet. "He accused me of stealing. You know how I feel about being called a thief."

"What if he apologized?"

She scoffed. "It's been three days. I doubt that's going to happen." He was probably waiting for *her* to apologize, since his damn mongoose convinced him she stole the amulet. She'd apologize for lying—she'd already said she was sorry for that—but she refused to apologize for something she didn't do.

"I don't know. The guy looked rough when I saw him. Red-rimmed eyes and everything." She spun the dial, entering the combination.

Alice waved her hand. "Allergies. Springtime in the Hill Country can be killer."

"If you say so."

There was no point in wondering what she'd do if he apologized. She hadn't seen hide nor tail of the man since he left her apartment in a huff. Never mind the fact she'd had a helping of rocky road ice cream every day since he left. She had to fill the hole he'd torn in her heart somehow, and thickening her waistline was the easiest way to do it.

She glanced at the clock. "Oh shoot. Daisy is holding a book for me at the library, but they close in five minutes. Do you mind...?"

"Go ahead." Megan closed the safe. "I'll lock up."

"Thanks. You're the best."

She tossed her hair behind her shoulder. "I know."

Alice hot-footed it across the square toward the library. The next installment in her favorite romance series hit the shelves today, and Daisy had promised to put it on hold for her. The balmy air signaled summer's fast approach, but the sun had already dipped behind the buildings, casting long shadows across the pavement and making the temperature downright pleasant.

She passed The Crow's Nest, waving to her mom through the window, and her long strides turned into a jog as she rounded the corner. The book would be the perfect distraction for her tonight. Gods knew she didn't need another evening wallowing in self-pity and missing Donovan Drake. She would get over that man if she had to pluck her own tail feathers to keep him off her mind.

She reached the library as Daisy stepped through the front door. With her curly red hair swept up in a twist and the black pencil skirt with low heels she wore, the possum shifter looked every bit the conservative librarian. How odd, though, that her arm was in a sling.

"Alice, you almost missed me. Come on in, and I'll get your book." She held the door open for her to enter.

"What happened to your arm?" Alice stepped inside and waited as Daisy closed the door.

"I fell off my bike yesterday." She laughed. "Rode it straight into a ditch and snapped my wrist in two places."

"Jeez, girl. Why haven't you gone down to the creek? That's got to hurt."

Daisy took the book from a shelf behind the counter and handed it to Alice, her red lips bowing into a frown. "That's the first thing I did."

A sinking sensation formed in her stomach. "It didn't heal you?"

"Not even a bit. I waded in and sat with the water up to my neck for half an hour. Nothing. I had to go to the hospital with the mundies and get a cast. Can you believe it?" She unhooked the clip from her hair and shook her head. "And I'm not the only one. Carson's girlfriend slammed a car door on his hand, breaking three of his fingers. Now he's wearing a splint."

"Oh no. It's worse than I thought." If the creek didn't heal her in that much time, the magic must have skedaddled. *Poop on a pancake!*

"I heard Christine was going to New York to try and force a meeting with Matthias. How did that go?"

Alice shook her head. "He refused to see her. She even tried following him when he left the office, but his bodyguards caught her. She's lucky they let her go without a fight. Hawks might rule the skies around here, but I can't imagine what a pack of angry wolf shifters could do to her."

"Kentucky Fried Hawk, that's what." Daisy stepped around the counter. "Shoot. If he would just come and read the damn book for us. Maybe there's a clue inside, and we don't need one of them to live here after all."

"There's got to be a way to read it without a Rainecourt."

"The magic is impenetrable."

Alice tapped a finger against her lips. No magic was completely impenetrable. Spells could be broken with the right knowledge and tools. "Maybe it's not magic masking the writing. What if it was written in invisible ink?"

Daisy shook her head. "I thought of that. I went all *National Treasure* on it and tried lemon juice and a hair dryer. It's either magic that only allows a Rainecourt to view it, like the legend says, or it's a hoax, and the pages really are blank."

"I wonder if we sent it to Matthias if he would read it for us. He might be willing to do that, right? Just spend a bit of time reading and tell us what it says. That wouldn't inconvenience him too much."

"The magic won't allow it to leave this building. I tried."

"Not a hoax then." Alice held the novel to her chest. "We've hit enough dead ends to fill a graveyard." It was starting to look like dredging was the only option. If the magic really was gone, the mundies couldn't make things any worse.

"Thanks for holding the book for me. I hope your arm heals quickly."

"My pleasure. Let me know how it is. I haven't read that series yet."

"You mean I've read a book the *librarian* hasn't?" Alice attempted a laugh, but with the news she'd just received, she couldn't muster an ounce of humor.

Daisy smiled sadly. "I'm sure I've read hundreds that you haven't."

Alice walked to her apartment, her feet feeling like lead as she made her way down the street. First, she lost the man she loved, and now the creek had lost its magic. This novel releasing was the only good thing that had happened in the past three days, and she planned to devour it tonight. Heck, maybe she'd stay up all night and finish it in one go. It wasn't like she had anything else to do.

She stared at the ground on her trek across the square, only lifting her gaze as she stepped onto the sidewalk in front of her apartment.

She froze.

Donovan stood outside her door, a pained expression on his face, a dozen deep red roses in his hand.

CHAPTER FIFTEEN

Alice didn't know whether to smile or scowl. Her heart couldn't decide what to do either. First, it slammed against her chest with one solid whack, and then it seemed to stutter, unable to start. Once it got going again, it felt like her crow had turned into a hummingbird and was trying to break free from her ribcage.

She was mad at Donovan for accusing of her of theft, but seeing him there, hurt filling his eyes, sent a warm tingling sensation down her spine. The flowers suggested he'd come to apologize, but she had no intention of letting him off easy.

Stopping two feet in front of him, she crossed her arms. "What are you doing here?"

He held her gaze, his mouth opening and closing once, as if he wasn't sure where to begin. "I owe you an apology."

"Damn right you do. I'm not a thief."

"No, you're not. And I'm sorry I accused you of such. The only thing you've stolen from me is my heart." He offered her the flowers, and she took them, not because she'd forgiven him, but because she loved flowers, and these were the most gorgeous, full, richly colored roses she'd ever seen.

"Really?" She ran a finger across a velvety bloom. "I'd hoped it was freely given."

"It was. It still is if you'll have it. I took Marty's word over yours," he continued his apology, "and I should know better. I hope you can find it in your heart to forgive me for this."

"For this? You say it like there's more you need forgiveness for." She pressed her nose against the soft petals, inhaling the fragrant aroma. The man knew how to make an apology; she'd give him bonus points for that.

"There is plenty more." He lowered his gaze as if ashamed.

Uh oh. That didn't sound good. "You'd better come up." Alice opened the door, and Donovan followed her upstairs to her apartment. She gestured to the sofa in the open living area, and he sank onto the cushion while she filled a vase with water and arranged the roses in it.

"The flowers are beautiful. Thank you."

He nodded. "Even as I accused you, in my heart, I didn't believe it. But Marty has been with me since I was a teen, and he knows how important the amulet is to me. It's no excuse. I had no reason to believe you would steal from me."

Alice sat next to him, angling her body to face him. "We both know your familiar doesn't care for me."

"It's not you. It's…" He closed his eyes for a long blink and exhaled slowly. "Marty put the amulet in the trash because he didn't want me to have its power. He saw it on you the first time we met, but he kept the information to himself."

"When he motorboated me."

"Yes, and when you caught him trying to steal it back, he accused you of taking it to keep himself out of trouble. I'm so sorry, Alice. Marty is sorry too."

"I…" She gritted her teeth. He didn't deserve to be let off the hook so easily, but she was in love with the man, and he'd apologized. Wasn't that enough? Staying mad wouldn't help anyone. "I forgive you. Heck, I forgive Marty too." Holding a grudge against a familiar would be like holding one against a child. Their brains weren't as developed as an adult's.

"Thank you."

She rested her hand on top of his knee. "Why didn't Marty want you to have the amulet's power? All it does is let you swap magic with someone, right? Is it dangerous?"

Donovan swallowed hard. "I'm afraid this is where my transgressions get harder to forgive. I've omitted the truth, led you to believe things about me that aren't true, and I've lied."

She returned her hand to her own lap, a sense of dread sinking in her chest. That sounded a whole lot worse than her transgression of taking something from his trash and not telling him.

Of course, he had another life back in New York. Probably a family and a scrawny little chihuahua named Cujo too. He and his gorgeous wife went to the theater and the opera and ate snails and fish eggs and other disgusting delicacies only rich people liked. *Ugh. I am a homewrecker!* "You're married, aren't you?"

"No, it's much worse than that."

"What's worse than infidelity?" She gasped. "Do you live with your mother?"

"No, I told you she passed away when I was young."

"Right. Sorry." *Way to go, Alice.* She clamped her mouth shut because a closed mouth gathered no feet—and she might never get the taste of rubber off her tongue now. In her defense, yes, he'd mentioned both his parents were deceased, but she not-so-conveniently forgot that little tidbit of info because he always clammed up when she asked him about his past.

"It's okay." He laced his fingers together. "Marty didn't want me to have the amulet's power because he was afraid he would lose me if I used it as I intended and was successful."

Alice chewed the inside of her cheek as she tried to understand what he was saying. Normally, the formality of his speech was an endearing quality, but damn... She felt like she was listening to a politician admit he'd been caught storing his sausage in an intern's cookie jar. "Spit it out, Donovan. You're skirting around the edges of what you're trying to tell me. Just say it, for heaven's sake."

"Here, I want you to have it." He pulled the amulet from his pocket and pressed it into her hand. "I don't have access to any magic of my own. When the creek didn't heal me, I planned to use the amulet, and Marty was afraid I'd abandon him if I succeeded."

What the what? He didn't...? But he... "Come again?"

"I don't have powers."

"Wait." She scratched her head. "So that story you told the game warden was true?"

"Every word of it."

"I am so confused."

"As I told the warden, I was born with my magic

locked. I trained. I learned spell-casting and everything that is required of the most powerful of warlocks, but I've never been successful. Not once." He ground his teeth.

Alice's mouth hung open, so she snapped it shut. Her mind reeled, her thoughts running a thousand miles a minute. "But your aura is so strong."

"A cloaking artifact."

"And you have a familiar. How did you...?"

"When it became evident my magic would never be unlocked, my father bought him on the black market and gave him to me for my fifteenth birthday."

"Oh. That was nice, I guess?" Black market familiars. She'd had no idea they existed, and her stomach soured at the thought of what else one might be able to buy in the shadows.

"Not in the slightest. It was meant as a rub. A constant reminder that a small animal was more magical than me. I'm only glad Marty and I bonded, and I was able to keep him from the torture he'd endured with his former owner."

"Poor Marty. Jeez Louise..." She shook her head. "Why didn't you want me to know?"

"No one besides my family knows. I've been forced to hide my incompetence my entire life, so I went into dealing magical artifacts to compensate for my inability. I'm a fraud, Alice, and I've never been more ashamed."

"You're not incompetent. There are plenty of other areas in life where you're successful. Magic isn't everything." Was she hurt that he'd kept it from her? Sure. But from what he'd told her about his childhood, she could understand why he'd be embarrassed. Heck, she'd been embarrassed about her occupation for a hot minute there too.

"It is everything in my family. So much so that I came here with the amulet, intent on using it to take the magic from the creek and keep it as my own."

Wait... Did he just say what she thought he said? That he was planning to *take* the town's magic? *Oh heck no.*

"Who's the thief now?" She shot to her feet, clenching her fist around the necklace. "You did it, didn't you? That's why the creek wouldn't heal Daisy. You stole its magic!"

"No, Alice. I didn't. I couldn't. Once I realized how much the creek means to this town...how much this town means to you...I couldn't go through with it."

She narrowed her eyes, studying him, not detecting an ounce of dishonesty in his words. Then again, that wasn't saying much. Even when he'd pretended to cast a healing spell on the creek, he'd pulled the wool over her eyes as easily as slipping on a fleece sweater. Love had blinded her.

"You have no reason to trust me," he said, "but I swear on my mother's grave I did not even attempt to take the magic from the creek."

She did believe him. Logically, she probably shouldn't have. Her mind said the reason the creek didn't heal Daisy was because the magic was stolen, but instinct, her crow, heck, everything inside her insisted Donovan wasn't to blame. She felt it in her bones. Plus, he'd just sworn on his own mother's grave. "I believe you," she whispered.

His posture relaxed. "Thank you."

"How did your mom die? You never told me anything about her."

"A drug overdose." He fisted his hands on his knees. "It happened when I was a baby."

"I'm so sorry."

He shook his head. "I never knew her. My birth was the result of my father's indiscretion with a prostitute." He laughed dryly. "Another fact he liked to remind me of regularly. I'm a stain on the family name."

"Your dad sounds like a piece of work."

He slid off the sofa onto both knees, taking her hands in his. "I'm sorry, Alice. I'm sorry I deceived you, and I'm sorry I didn't trust you to accept me without my magic. I was a fool, and I don't deserve you."

"I don't know about all that." She sat on the couch and tugged him up next to her. "If you want my pair of pennies on the subject…"

"Of course."

"Stop trying to be someone you're not. You're a kind, sweet, sensitive man, and people will love you for you, whether you have powers or not. I know I do." *Oops.* She just said that out loud, didn't she?

Donovan's lips twitched like he was suppressing a smile. "Does this mean I'm forgiven for both the accusation and the deception?"

She rolled her eyes, more at herself than at him. Under normal circumstances, she'd have let him grovel a little longer, but she was just so damn thrilled to have him back, she couldn't help herself. Besides… "We all make mistakes. Heck, the reason I'm so sensitive about being called a thief is because I used to be one."

"Oh?"

She shrugged. "When Megan and I were teenagers, we had no qualms with taking things right from people's front porches. We hadn't quite learned how to control our animal instincts…until the town sheriff set us straight."

"You never stop surprising me." He grinned.

"We were minors, so that part of my police record is sealed. Anyway, the point is, I forgive you. But you have to promise me that there will be no more secrets. If you want to be with me, I'm not willing to accept anything less than total honesty."

He swallowed again, his lips flattening into a line.

"You're not done telling me everything, are you?" Wariness drew out her words.

"There is one more thing…"

There was no point in beating around the bush. Thus far, she'd forgiven him, so he might as well spit it out.

Alice sat next to him, her body angled toward his, her smile fading the longer he hesitated. "What is it?"

"Marcus Rainecourt was my father." He held his breath, waiting for the anger to ignite in her eyes. For her to swear he should never show his face in Shift Creek again. He deserved nothing less.

Her lips parted on a quick intake of breath, and her brow furrowed before rising and then furrowing again. "But your last name is Drake."

"From my mother."

Her lips moved as if her thoughts raced too quickly for her to speak. He deserved to be berated. If she threw him out and never wanted to see him again, he'd understand. Instead, she smiled.

"This is amazing!"

He chuckled, relieved. "That is not the reaction I was expecting, but I'll take it."

"I mean, I'd have preferred if you told me from the get-go, but it's not too late. You can still save the creek." Her eyes brightened as her smile widened.

How he hated to burst her bubble of elation, but he'd promised nothing but the truth. "I don't see how I could.

My presence in the town hasn't helped. I've bathed in it on multiple occasions, including the last full moon. It recognizes me as human."

"Maybe so, but we've got a secret weapon. There's a book in the library, written by the warlock who blessed the creek himself. It's enchanted so that only someone from his family can read the pages. They appear blank to everyone else, but *you* can read it, Donovan. Surely it will have the answer. If anything, we'll know for certain how our magical town came to be and if there's anything we can do to save it."

"I don't hold much hope in that. Whatever Rainecourt magic I have, it's locked deep inside me. If the creek didn't recognize it…"

"Hope is all I have left. The full moon is next week. Then the mundies are going to dredge, and it will all be over. We might as well change the town's name to Mundy Creek since the magic is all but gone."

Hope. He'd come to Texas full of hope, but he hadn't found what he was looking for. Instead, he'd found a love he never dreamed he'd achieve. A woman who accepted him for who he was. "Well, then. Let's go to the library."

"It's closed. They open tomorrow at ten."

"We'll go tomorrow at ten." He did his best to reassure her with his eyes. He highly doubted the pages would reveal themselves to him, but if Alice could hold on to hope, so could he.

She scooted closer, resting her hand on his thigh. "I've missed you."

"I never knew it was possible to miss someone as much as I've missed you." He cupped her cheek in his hand. "I'm so sorry."

"I've forgiven you, so you can stop apologizing."

"Perhaps I haven't forgiven myself."

She placed her hand over his, nuzzling into his palm. "Work on that on your own time, okay?"

"I will."

She drifted toward him, her gaze on his lips as she paused a few inches from her destination. "You should kiss me now."

Without hesitation, he closed the space between them, claiming the prize he would never deserve, yet would cherish for as long as he walked this earth.

Her lips were softer than rose petals, and as her fingers tightened on his thigh, he placed his hand on her lower back, tugging her even closer. She responded to his touch as if she could read his mind, sliding her hands behind his neck and leaning into the kiss, her tongue tangling with his as she straddled his lap.

Heat built in his core, cascading downward to pool in his groin. She rocked her hips, grinding against him, and he couldn't stop the moan from rumbling in his chest. "You are the sexiest woman alive."

She grinned slyly and peeled her shirt over her head to reveal an emerald green bra trimmed in lace. "How about now?"

"If you get any hotter, I may spontaneously combust."

Reaching behind her back, she unfastened her bra and tossed it aside. Donovan's core tightened, and what little blood was left in his head rushed to his dick. He glided his fingers down her chest, gently brushing her nipples, reveling in her quick intake of breath and the goosebumps forming on her skin.

Leaning forward, he sucked her into his mouth, teasing her with his tongue until she hardened into a pearl. She tangled her fingers in his hair and let out an erotic moan that wrapped around him like a silk scarf, tying him up in passion.

Her hands trembled as she undid the buttons on his shirt, and he moved his lips to her other breast. With this nipple pleasantly hardened, he straightened, gazing into the depths of her green eyes.

She laid open his shirt and ran her fingers down his chest. Then, she leaned forward and pressed her lips to his scar, an act so tender, so gentle, he nearly choked on a sob.

"You'll tell me about this later."

"Yes." His voice came out as a whisper. He would tell her anything. *Do* anything for her.

She slid off the couch and shimmied out of the rest of her clothes before removing his and returning to his lap. Wrapping her fingers around his dick, she guided him to her folds, and as she enveloped him, she uttered the most beautiful phrase he'd ever heard. "I love you, Donovan."

His entire body shuddered at her words. No one—in his entire life—had ever said that to him.

"I love you, Alice." Sliding his fingers into her silky hair, he pulled her to him, crushing his mouth to hers.

She moved, sliding up and down his dick, the warmth of her embrace pushing him closer and closer to the edge. Slipping his hand between her legs, he pressed his thumb against her sweet spot and moved it in circles until she cried out.

The sound of his name on her lips consumed him, and the orgasm ripped through his body, setting every nerve on fire as she rode him. As her movements slowed, the flames calmed to burning embers, her warm breath against his neck fanning to keep them lit.

Her breathing eased, and she kissed him gently before leaning back. "Everything makes sense now."

"What do you mean?" He tucked her hair behind her ear.

"The connection between us, the way we feel about each other... I thought it felt instinctual, and it does. If you're a Rainecourt, you have shifter blood. My crow has bonded with you."

"An unbreakable bond, I hope?"

She grinned. "Crows mate for life."

Exactly the words he wanted to hear. He pulled her in for another kiss, losing himself in her embrace.

As the kiss slowed to a soft brush of the lips, she straightened and ran her fingers over his scar. "Who did this?"

"I think you know." He placed his hand over hers, holding it against his chest.

"Marcus." She shook her head. "But why?"

"He thought he could bring out my powers by threatening my life. I was supposed to defend myself as he hurled magic at me. This one nearly killed me."

"How old were you?"

"Twelve."

"That's downright awful. I used to feel bad for hating a man I've never met, but not anymore. *He's* the stain on your family name. Not you."

"Considering what he's done to this town, I have to agree." He closed his fingers around her hand. "Do you understand why I was hesitant to tell you who I really am? I was afraid you'd dismiss me immediately if you knew whose blood I carry in my veins."

"I'd like to think I'd have given you a chance, but I probably wouldn't have." She shrugged. "I can be a little judgy where the rich and powerful are concerned. I'll try to work on that."

"May I stay the night?"

"Will Marty be okay alone?"

"He'll be fine. I'll go home in the morning and bring him with us to the library. He has his own apologies to make."

CHAPTER SIXTEEN

A lice leaned on the counter in the library as Daisy rotated her wrist. Shifters healed faster than mundies, thankfully. She'd removed the cast this morning and, by tomorrow, she would be right as a rainstorm.

"This is the longest I've ever gone with an injury," Daisy said. "I really hope Donovan can read the book, because pain is not fun."

"I hear you." The five minutes it took Alice to fly to the creek after her squabble with the trap were excruciating. She couldn't imagine dealing with the agony for days.

"You told him what the other warlocks said, right? About how the magic is tied to the family? I still don't get why he didn't say something sooner."

Alice ran her finger over the binding of the book that could save them all. "That's mostly my fault. I didn't have anything nice to say about his dad, so I should have kept my mouth shut. But, you know me…"

"Well, we know who he is now. That's what's important." She opened the book return bin and took out a stack of novels, setting them next to the computer. "And you two are an item. It's funny how it's come full circle. A powerful warlock blessed the creek and married a crow shifter…and now it's happening again."

"I don't want to count my chicks before the eggs are even laid, but…it is romantic, isn't it?" Of course, Daisy didn't know the secret about Donovan's magic—or lack thereof—and Alice wasn't about to spill it. Their stories didn't run exactly parallel, since Alice's warlock couldn't fix the creek himself, but he was *her* warlock now. And that made her heart sing.

Daisy scanned the barcode on the back of a book and cut her gaze toward the entrance as the door chimed. "Oh, is that him? He's cute!"

Alice smiled as Donovan strode toward her, and a thousand butterflies flitted in her stomach. He wore dark jeans and a lavender button-up that contrasted with his dark eyes in an oh-so-sexy way. He kissed her on the cheek and rested a hand on his satchel. "Hello again."

"It's been a minute, hasn't it?" She laughed. "This is Daisy. She's a possum shifter and the town's head librarian."

"Pleasure to meet you, Daisy." He shook her hand, and she giggled like a schoolgirl.

Honestly, Alice couldn't blame her. Donovan had that effect on people. "Can you lock the doors for a bit? I'd hate for a mundy to walk in just as magic shoots from the pages."

"Good idea." Daisy grabbed a key ring and padded to the door.

Donovan opened his satchel and lifted Marty from inside. "I believe you have something to say to Alice?"

"I'm sorry," he sulked.

Alice fought her smile.

"Continue," Donovan said with all the authority of a father making his son apologize for throwing a baseball through her window.

"I shouldn't have blamed you for taking the necklace, and I'm sorry for trying to keep you apart." He climbed up Donovan's arm and balanced on his shoulder. "You make him happy, and that makes me happy, and I'm sorry for making *you* unhappy."

"For a familiar, you're very good at apologies."

Donovan patted his head. "He learned from the best."

"You're forgiven," Alice said. "I hope we can become friends."

"Me too." Marty bared his teeth—which must have been his attempt at a smile—but the sharp, jagged line of white reminded her more of the creepy clown from *It* than an adorable animal.

She wasn't sure if she should laugh or shudder, so she pressed her lips together, trying to keep a neutral expression.

"Oh, and I actually like pets," he said, "so any time you feel like giving me a scratch, go for it."

"I'll keep that in mind."

"All clear." Daisy picked up the book and carried it to a table in between the bookshelves. "I'll give you two some privacy, but you have to promise to tell me what it says."

"Thanks, Daisy." Alice settled into a chair next to Donovan and gazed at the book.

The simple brown binding was unremarkable, and the volume couldn't have held more than fifty pages. It was hard to believe such a nondescript little book could be the secret weapon that saved the creek, but she crossed her fingers, hoping to high heaven it was.

Donovan placed his hands on either side of the book

and pressed his lips into a hard line. "If magic is required to bring out the ink, I…"

She put her hand on top of his. "I know. Let's just see what happens."

He nodded and opened it to the first page, while Alice braced herself for a blast of light to shoot from the paper or a cloud of glitter to puff up in front of them…*something* to indicate the magical seal had been broken. Even shifters sparkled when they activated their power, so an enchanted book should have emitted some sort of light or sound.

Sadly, it was as plain as a piece of buttered white bread…not even the honey butter kind either. Plain ol' unsalted butter. No, worse. Margarine.

She sighed. "It was worth a shot."

Donovan glanced at her before returning his gaze to the book. "A Magical History of Shift Creek as Recorded by Cyrus Rainecourt, Master Warlock, and Beatrice Monroe, Crow Shifter."

Alice's mouth hung open as she stared at the blank page. "You're joking, right?"

He gave her a quizzical look. "What would I be joking about? That's what it says right here." He pointed.

"I don't see anything." Excitement coiled in her muscles, making her blood hum. "Turn the page."

Donovan flipped a few pages, his eyes scanning them from top to bottom. "It explains how Cyrus and Beatrice met and how the creek came to be enchanted."

Marty hopped from Donovan's shoulder to hers, his little claws digging into her shirt. "I'm with Alice, boss. Those pages are blank."

She ran a finger down the familiar's side. His fur was coarse like a short-haired terrier's, and he stretched his

FLIPPING THE BIRD | 167

body, closing his eyes like he enjoyed it. He'd missed out on so many pets by being a little doo-doo head.

Donovan's smile could have lit an entire city block. "They're not blank to me."

Alice was tempted to pluck Marty from her shoulder and set him on the table. His claws must have been doing a number on her shirt, but she didn't dare reject him when he'd finally accepted her. "What does it say?"

"Cyrus was an artifacts dealer like me." He laughed. "He was passing through Texas on his way to acquire a relic."

"What kind of relic?"

"It doesn't say." He turned the page, and Alice held her breath as he scanned the contents. "On his journey, he came across an injured crow. He used healing magic to restore her health, and she transformed into a woman named Beatrice."

Alice gasped. "The crow shifter he married."

He scanned a few more pages, nodding. "Beatrice brought him to the town to help the others. All of the shifters had contracted a mysterious disease, and several had died."

"Disease? How can that be since we're immune? Heck, we don't even catch colds. The only things shifters ever die of are accidents and old age."

Donovan held up a finger, practically shushing her. She would have been annoyed—and told him so—under any other circumstances, but she was so excited to find out what else the book said, she might molt if he didn't hurry up and tell her.

After reading a few more pages, he looked at her. "Another warlock had poisoned the creek when the shifters refused to accept him as their leader. It was the town's main water source."

"That bastard turkey! They didn't have the same water purifying systems we have now, either."

"Filters wouldn't have helped. It was magically poisoned." He continued reading. "I need to find out how Cyrus extracted the poison and what spell he used to bless the stream. Give me a minute; there's a lot of superfluous information in here."

Marty finally hopped off her shoulder and lay on the table in front of her. She stroked his fur, and he rolled onto his back, letting her scratch his belly. He sure was cute when he wasn't being a butt…or trying to smile.

She waited what felt like a million excruciating minutes while Donovan read. Finally, after the under-world froze over and thawed out again, he tapped the page.

"There were too many sick for him to heal them all. Performing magic can be taxing on a body, and it requires rest to recover when you cast powerful spells such as the one that cured the illness. That's why he gave the creek healing powers."

"So it was a healing spell on the water?"

He shook his head. "The stream was too far gone for that. He performed a sacrificial spell."

"It sounds self-explanatory, but can you explain anyway?"

Donovan sat up straight, an expression of awe in his eyes as he stared straight ahead for a moment before looking at her. "He gave up his healing magic to save the town and instilled it in the creek so that all could access it without the limitations of his mortal body."

"Wow. Now there's a selfless act for you. He was just

passing through, and he gave up a part of himself to help a bunch of shifters he hardly knew?"

He took her hand, lacing their fingers together. "He was in love with Beatrice, so it makes perfect sense. He would do anything for love."

"But he won't do that," Alice sang.

Donovan furrowed his brow. "What won't he do?"

"No, it's a song. Meatloaf?"

"Is that what you want for dinner?"

"The song is called 'I Would Do Anything for Love…'" Alice laughed. She'd have to school him in music when this was done. "Never mind. So he gave up his magic to save the creek. How is it tied to the family, then?"

"In order for the magic to remain, every thirty years, a Rainecourt must cast a healing spell to replenish the magic."

"So they don't have to live here? Just cast a spell and get on with their lives, and the town will prosper?"

He turned the page and read some more. "Part of the sacrifice was his promise that his family would stay in the town and tend to the creek. The spirit of the stream accepted his offer, so any Rainecourt born outside of Shift Creek would be born with their magic locked. The only way to unlock their power would be to bathe in the stream while it's flowing in reverse."

Her eyes widened as she shook her head. "That explains why you don't have powers."

"And why the creek did nothing to help me."

"Does it say how to fix it?"

"The incantation is here." He pointed to the blank page. "I assume my father knew about and ignored the family obligation when his wife died."

"And he kept it a secret from you and your brothers."
That self-centered stick of jerky.

"Leaving the estate to me was the final nail in the town's coffin. I can't cast this spell." He brought a heavy fist down on the table. "If he'd given the property to Griffin, the problem would be fixed by now."

She squeezed his hand. "There's still a chance he'll get your message."

"In three days? It's doubtful, and even if he does check in, it will take days to travel to an airport. He goes deep into uncharted territory on his missions."

She chewed the inside of her cheek. He had a point. "What about Matthias? I know you don't have a good relationship, but…"

"I called him. He refused, saying it was nothing more than a marketing ploy."

She slumped. "Like father, like son."

"Precisely." He turned the page and continued reading. "Oh. This is not good."

"What does it say?"

"Should the magic be allowed to run out, someone with Rainecourt blood must perform a personal sacrifice under a full moon to restore it. Otherwise, the poison will return. The spell Cyrus cast suppressed it, but he wasn't able to completely remove it."

"The poison? As in…we'll all kick the bucket?"

He squinted at the page. "It seems so."

"Oh, hell."

Donovan cut his gaze toward her and lifted a brow.

"What? Sometimes a situation requires a well-placed curse." She straightened. "Any chance Griffin would give up some of his magic to help a bunch of strangers?"

"Absolutely none."

She sank in her chair, and Marty climbed up her arm to nuzzle her neck. "So that's it, then. No more magical creek. No more tourists. No more town. The thing we've built our livelihoods on is going to kill us if we stay."

Donovan drummed his fingers on the table, and Marty hopped to his shoulder to whisper in his ear.

"I had the same idea." Donovan ground his teeth. "But which one?"

"Which one what? You guys wanna keep the lady in the room informed?"

Marty climbed down his arm to stand on the table. "It's gotta be this one." He tapped the bracelet on Donovan's wrist.

Donovan closed his eyes and let out a slow exhale. "You're right." He turned to Alice. "I don't have magic of my own to sacrifice, but I do have magical artifacts. I'll offer the one I hold most dear."

He slipped the bracelet off, laying it on the table, and the deep-orange glow of his aura faded to the color of a pearl, barely shimmering at all. Alice squeezed her eyes shut, blinking as she opened them again, but the magic in his aura had all but faded to nothing.

"It's my aura-cloaking coin. It's what I use to fake the appearance of magic. Most of the time, objects like this are used to infiltrate a pack or coven, but I use it to make myself into someone I'm not."

"Didn't you say it was a gift from your father?"

"It was." He laughed dryly. "He forced me to wear it at all times to avoid bringing the family any more embarrassment should my true lineage ever be discovered. I could have stopped, but everyone I know believes I have magic."

She took his hand. Seeing the pain in his eyes was unbearable. "I'm sure a different artifact would work, right? Is there something else that would be a sacrifice for you to give up?"

"It must be this. I have a chance at a new life here, and I will start it with honesty." He clasped her hand between both of his. "Besides, I would gladly give up all my magic to save this town. Having you in my life is all I need."

Marty cleared his throat.

Donovan laughed. "And you, old friend."

"Do you think it will work?" Alice asked.

"It has to."

She pursed her lips, trying to ignore the doubt rumbling in her stomach. Or maybe that was just hunger pangs. A growl rose up from her core. Yep, she was hungry. "You're right. It does. You have Rainecourt blood; you'll be making a sacrifice. It'll work." She rose to her feet. "I'll let the committee know we've found the solution. They're going to be so thrilled."

His eyes tightened. "I would prefer to perform the sacrifice without an audience. If it doesn't work, I… Living my life as a mundy will take some adjustment."

She giggled at his use of their word. "Baby steps. Got it. I won't tell them until it's done. They'll be up at the springs that night, so we can do it where the creek cuts through your property."

"Thank you for understanding."

"Sounds like we've got a date beneath the full moon. In the meantime, let's grab lunch. Talking about Meatloaf has made me hungry."

CHAPTER SEVENTEEN

The full moon hung high in the sky, not a cloud in sight to obscure it from view. It taunted them as Alice walked by Donovan's side toward the creek with Marty clinging to his shoulder. As if they needed a reminder this was their absolute last chance to restore the magic and save the town.

"I really hope this works." She stumbled in the grass.

Donovan caught her by the arms, holding her steady, and looked into her eyes. "It will. My heritage alone was enough to allow me to read the book. Until that day in the library, I hadn't removed the bracelet since I was twelve years old. It's as much a part of me as the nose on my face."

"Is it your real nose? It looks too perfect to be your real nose." It was flawlessly straight, not a single bump or scar in sight. Heck, even his pores were nearly invisible, which was so unfair. "You didn't have some kind of magical plastic surgery to change your looks?"

"I've faked a lot of things in my life, but my appearance is mine alone. I've done nothing to alter it."

She narrowed her eyes. "What else have you faked?"

He laughed. "Nothing with you, aside from my magic."

Her brow arched as she studied him. "Nothing... bedroom-wise? You promise?"

"Never. You can light me ablaze with a simple look. I've told you my truth, and I will never deceive you again, especially in the bedroom."

"Or on the kitchen counter? Or over the bathroom sink?"

"I promise."

Marty covered his ears. "TMI, you guys. Seriously."

They paused on the edge of the bank, the cool spring breeze raising goosebumps on Alice's arms. Capris and a tank top weren't the best choice of eveningwear, but it had been so warm during the day, she didn't think to change. Donovan's amulet rested against her chest—she could actually wear it on the outside of her shirt now that the whole dumpster-diving ordeal had been aired out—and she wore a pair of black patent leather sandals. Also not a good choice for traipsing through a field in the dark, but hey...she was used to flying to places like this.

Donovan kicked off his shoes and pulled off his socks, stuffing them inside. Standing barefoot in the grass, he closed his eyes and inhaled deeply, angling his face toward the moon.

"What are you doing?" Alice asked.

"He's getting in the zone," Marty replied.

Donovan grinned and opened one eye to glance at her. "I'm connecting with nature and the spirit of the land. I'll do the same when I enter the river, connecting with her spirit before offering the sacrifice."

"Gotcha. I'll zip it and let you do your thing." Being

part animal, Alice felt a constant connection to nature, but she could see how someone who was mostly human would need to take a moment to get out of their head.

Clutching the bracelet in his hand, Donovan waded into the center of the creek. He stood still, closing his eyes again as the stream slowly flowed around him. Alice dropped to her knees, silently praying to the spirit of the creek and every god in existence that this sacrifice would be enough.

Somewhere, deep in her bones, she knew it wouldn't be, but she begged to be wrong. Heck, she'd never wanted to be *more* wrong in her entire life. Not even back in high school when she'd been sure her parents were planning to pack up and move to The Netherlands after she eavesdropped on their conversation. As it turned out, they'd only bought a Dutch oven for the restaurant. Lordy, lordy, Alice had been happy to be wrong about that! Hopefully this situation would be a replay.

Donovan lifted the bracelet toward the moon, his voice resonating deep and powerful, "I call on you, the spirit of Shift Creek. Please accept this sacrifice of magic from a Rainecourt warlock and restore your healing properties."

He plunged the artifact into the water, holding it beneath the surface as his eyes closed and he chanted what sounded like a prayer. Or maybe he was trying one last spell. Who knew? He spoke too quietly for Alice to understand his words.

She stared at the stream, squinting at the water around him and holding her breath as she waited for something to happen. But the water didn't sparkle or shimmer or even bubble a little to indicate it had accepted Donovan's sacrifice.

"I beg of you. I have nothing else to offer." Donovan opened his hand, allowing the bracelet to sink to the bottom of the creek. Still nothing happened.

He looked at Alice, a sadness in his eyes so palpable, she choked on a sob. Then he whispered again, resting his hands on the surface of the water, but the creek didn't respond to his plea.

He clenched his fists. "If you won't accept my offer, then take my life."

Alice gasped. "Donovan, no!" *Holy mother of crazy!* The man had gone cuckoo. "We'll move. The people of this town will survive elsewhere. You don't have to die to save us."

"Take me! Take my magic!" Marty scurried to the edge of the bank. "I'll be a regular mongoose. I don't mind." He tapped Alice on the knee, looking at her expectantly, as if he wanted her to pick him up and toss him to Donovan.

These two were a big ol' jar of mixed nuts…roasted and salted.

"Absolutely not," Donovan said. "I'm sorry, Alice. The creek requires a *personal* magical sacrifice, and I simply have nothing to offer that will suffice. I've done all I can."

Alice swallowed the lump that had formed in her throat. Heaven have mercy, she was really about to do this. She had no other choice, though, did she? Not if she wanted to save her home. "You have, but I haven't."

She rose to her feet, slipping out of her sandals and wiggling her toes in the grass. She'd never consciously tried to connect with nature, but it wouldn't hurt for what she was about to do.

Scooping the amulet into her palm, she inhaled a shaky breath. "You can sacrifice my crow." Who was the nut job now? "I'll flip her to you, and you can offer her to the creek."

"Alice, no. Don't be ridiculous."

"Ridiculous?" Her voice cracked. "You can sacrifice your life, but it's ridiculous for me to offer my crow? Do you hear yourself?"

"I offered my life in a tantrum. I knew it wouldn't be accepted."

"Did you?"

He clenched his teeth. "No, not really." He cut his gaze to Marty before returning to her eyes. "It's my magic that must be sacrificed. The creek won't accept yours."

"It will. We're connected, you and me. My crow has bonded with you, remember? She's a part of you, as you're a part of me."

"Your crow is who you are."

"It's part of who I am, but it's not all of me."

He shook his head and moved toward her. "I won't let you sacrifice yourself for my shortcomings."

Alice fisted her hands on her hips. "You don't get to make that decision, mister. I'm going to flip you my bird, and you're going to give her to the creek. End of story."

"Alice…"

"I can save the creek. Let me." She straightened her spine. "Take my crow."

Her chest burned, electricity shooting down to her toes as her crow magic broke free from her body. Donovan stiffened, and his aura sparkled green before he transformed into her crow right above the water.

She should have considered the fact Donovan hadn't practiced using her wings like Megan had because, boy, oh boy, making him shift over the water was a mistake.

He flapped wildly, the wings picking up water as they

slapped the surface, soaking the feathers through and weighing him down. If he thought flying dry was difficult, flying wet was like moving through a Jell-O mold. He went under, his beak breaking the surface and letting out a grating caw as he flailed.

"Crap on a cracker. I should've taught you to fly first." Without its magical properties, the creek would drown him. Alice jumped into the water, her feet sinking into the gooey mud near the bank. "Ick!"

She sloshed her way to the center of the creek and plucked Donovan from the stream, holding him—her crow—in both her hands. He shook, sending droplets flying into her face.

Alice sputtered and lifted a shoulder to wipe her eye. "Give her to the creek."

He looked at her, cocking his little head, and cawed.

"Please."

With a nod, he used her hands as a springboard and dove beak-first into the water. Golden light flashed beneath the surface. A single, bowling ball-sized bubble rose to the top and popped. Silence.

Alice's heart lodged in her throat, and she plunged her hands into the creek, frantically searching either for her crow or the man, whichever form Donovan was in.

"Where is he?" Marty called from the bank.

"I don't know." She spun in a circle and dropped to her knees, reaching her hands into the water all around her. "You better not have taken both my crow and my boyfriend! He didn't mean it when he offered his life."

Tears filled her eyes as she slipped on the muddy bottom, scrambling to her feet. "Please."

The water in front of her pulled away as if one tiny

section of the creek was shifting flow. Then it swirled in a glittering whirlpool of magic.

The surface broke, and Donovan shot up, gasping for breath as a wave rushed toward them. The impact knocked Alice off her feet. She went under, the force of the flow carrying her downstream until her back met a massive rock.

She fought to right herself, but the water flowing over her head held her down. She couldn't breathe, and at this point, a normal person would have panicked. But a sense of calm washed over her instead. Yep, she'd definitely earned a place in the mixed nut jar.

As she gazed toward the surface above, she could just make out the light of the moon. Then, to add to the crazy, the water seemed to gather in the light, forming the image of a woman's face.

This was it. The lack of oxygen to her brain was making her hallucinate. It wouldn't be long now before she gave the bucket the boot. *Please let me get out of this alive. Donovan and I will live as mundies for the rest of our lives if you'll spare us and the town.*

The woman's face in the water smiled. *"Your sacrifice has been accepted. A healing spell must be cast upon the creek, and all will be as it was."*

A healing spell? *Fan-friggin-tastic.* Who was supposed to cast the spell when Donovan didn't have any powers?

As the face dissipated, fingers wrapped around Alice's arms, jerking her from the water. Her head lolled back as Donovan cradled her against his chest and plowed through the creek toward the bank. He laid her in the grass before climbing out and kneeling by her side.

"Alice?" His voice sounded panicked, but as he rested his hand on her chest, he sighed with relief.

That meant she was breathing, right? She sure as heck hoped so.

"Is she okay?" Marty's tiny paws rested against her cheek.

"Alice, can you hear me?" Donovan ran his fingers over her forehead.

She blinked her eyes open, squinting as his handsome features came into view. He smiled, and the corners of his eyes crinkled.

They were alive, at least, but her chest ached like it had been cut open and scrambled with an electric mixer for real this time.

Her crow was gone forever.

Alice lifted her head, rising onto her elbows. "I'm okay." She would be, anyway. Maybe. "I had the weirdest dream, though. The spirit of the creek said you needed to cast a healing spell, but you can't..."

Donovan sat back on his heels, and she gasped at the sight of him. He no longer wore the bracelet that masked his translucent aura, but now he glowed a shimmering deep blue, like the ocean beneath a full moon.

She squeezed her eyes shut and opened them again. Surely she was seeing things after being underwater for so long, but nope. His aura glowed with powerful magic. "Do you see him like I do, Marty?"

The mongoose tilted his head. "You got your magic, boss!"

Donovan rose to his feet, tugging Alice up with him. "A healing spell, she said?"

"Unless I was imagining things."

He took her hand and raised his other toward the creek, speaking the same spell he'd pretended to cast before. Golden light ascended from the bottom to sparkle on the surface, and the level of the stream began to rise. Then, the most wonderful, beautiful sight Alice had ever seen appeared before her eyes.

The creek reversed its flow.

"Holy mother of shock and awe. You did it!" She threw her arms around Donovan and planted a big sloppy kiss right on his mouth.

Wrapping his arms behind her back, he lifted her from the ground, spinning in a circle and laughing before returning her feet to the ground. "*We* did it."

"We did, didn't we?" She watched the creek rise and flow, returning to its former glory, and shouts of joy drifted on the breeze from upstream.

"The committee sounds happy," Donovan said.

"The whole town will be celebrating tonight."

"Shall we join them?"

Alice shrugged. Happy as she was the town was saved, she didn't much feel like celebrating, what with the giant gaping hole in her soul and all. But she knew she should. "We can go for a little while."

She slipped her shoes back on her feet and cast one more glance at Shift Creek. As she turned toward the manor, a flash of green light caught her eye. An emerald sphere the size of a volleyball drifted toward her in the water.

Her limbs trembled as it rose from the surface, lighting in the air and transforming into…a crow.

She gasped.

With a flap of its translucent wings, it soared toward her, slamming into her chest and fusing with her soul.

"What the…? How…?" She pressed her hands to her body, expecting to find a hole where the bird might have torn her open, but it hadn't. It had made her whole.

Laughter bubbled from her throat as she looked at Donovan. He appeared just as shocked as she was.

She shifted and took to the sky, cawing with delight. Her feathers were soaked, and she felt like she was flying through mud, but she didn't care.

Alice had her crow.

CHAPTER EIGHTEEN

Donovan watched as Alice soared through the sky, her caws echoing on the spring breeze. She swooped toward him, rolling through the air before shooting upward again with the grace of a swan. The woman was magnificent.

He chuckled, shaking his head as he kneeled by the water. She'd be up there for a while, and who could blame her? She'd lost a part of herself. Even though her sacrifice had only lasted a few minutes, she was whole again.

Now that Donovan's magic had been unlocked, he could understand her elation. As Alice would say, *heck*, he could barely contain his own.

He whispered an illumination spell he'd learned as a child, and a ball of warm, white light formed in his palm. A giggle rolled up from his chest—not the manliest way to laugh, but he didn't give a damn. He had magic!

Closing his fist, he extinguished the light and gazed at the moon's reflection on the water. Shift Creek had changed him. He'd come with the intent of taking a magic that didn't belong to him, but in the end, he'd been willing to give it all up—his home in New York, his chance at having powers...everything—to restore the same magic he'd wanted to steal and to save this town.

All for the elegant black bird flying above him. This creek had been blessed for love, and love had revived it.

"I don't get it." Marty climbed up his arm to settle on his shoulder. "The book said you had to make a sacrifice, but you ended up with more than you gave."

"Many times, in magic, intent is the driving force. Perhaps the fact we were both willing to give up our powers and live as humans was enough to restore the spell." He ran a hand over the water, and golden magic sparkled on the surface. "I may have also promised to live here for the rest of my life with Alice and tend to the creek to keep it healthy."

"So this is our forever home?"

"It is."

Marty hopped to the ground and stood on his hind legs in front of Donovan. "And I can stay, even though you have powers now?"

He scratched the mongoose beneath his chin. "No one could ever replace you, Marty. You are my familiar."

Marty let out a relieved sigh as Alice landed next to them. She ruffled her feathers before a deep emerald light formed around her, and she shifted into human form.

"How was your flight?" Donovan asked as he rose to his feet.

"Fantastically awesome!" She took his face in her hands and kissed him. "Ten to one there's a party at The Crow's Nest. Wanna go so they can meet the man who rescued the town?"

"You mean the woman?"

"Both."

He wrapped his arms around her waist and brushed his lips to hers. "Perhaps we should make ourselves a little more presentable. I'm sure your parents wouldn't appreciate us dripping creek water all over the floor."

"They'd murder us." She grinned. "Race you to the house."

"On your mark, get set, go."

As Alice shifted to her crow and took off toward the manor, excitement fizzed in Donovan's chest. He recited a teleportation spell, and, in an instant, he found himself standing on the front porch.

"Not cool, boss," Marty shouted from the creek before scurrying through the grass toward the house.

Alice landed on the steps and shifted to human form, resting a hand on her hip. "That's cheating."

"You used your magic; I used mine."

"Okay, I guess that's fair. Let me get cleaned up. Good thing I left some clothes here." She strode into the manor.

Marty panted as he reached the front door. "Can I come to the party?"

"Of course." Donovan followed them inside.

***

Alice took a quick shower to wash the creek water from her hair before throwing on the jeans and t-shirt she'd left in one of Donovan's drawers. She blew out her hair until it was mostly dry and padded to the foyer to find Donovan standing with his hands clasped behind his back.

He wore dark jeans and a pale blue button-up, his thousand-watt smile brightening when he saw her. "You look beautiful."

"Thanks. Are you ready?"

186 | CARRIE PULKINEN

"Almost. Before we go, I need to ask you something."
He dropped to one knee, and Alice's heart took a quick
dip into her stomach before lodging in her throat.

Holy mother of happily ever afters! He hadn't even asked
the thing he was going to ask, and tears were already
welling in her eyes. She swallowed hard, sending her heart
back into her chest where it belonged. "What's this?"

He held out his hand, and a small black box appeared
in his palm. "I love you, Alice." He opened the box to
reveal a sparkling diamond set in white gold, with two
emeralds on either side of the stone. Shiny, just how she
liked things.

Her bottom lip trembled as her gaze bounced between
his dark eyes and the glittering ring.

"I made a promise to the creek that I would live here
forever and tend to her health. Will you do me the honor
of staying by my side?"

"Donovan..." Her stupid heart bounced back into her
throat, making her choke on a sob.

"Will you marry me, Alice?"

"Yes! Heck yes!"

He plucked the ring from the box and slid it on her
finger. "You've made me the happiest man alive."

"I don't think I've ever been this happy in my entire
life."

"I get it," Marty said. "Everybody's happy. Now, can
we please go to the party? I'm starving."

As Alice expected, The Crow's Nest was packed when
they arrived. Both mundies and supes alike filled the tables
and stood around the bar, mingling and laughing, celebrating as they should.

She spotted Christine and tugged Donovan through
the crowd toward the committee chair.

Megan stopped them before they could reach her. "Oh. My. Word." She gaped at Donovan. "Your aura has changed. And you…" She gripped Alice's shoulder. "You're absolutely glowing."

"I'm shiny too." She wiggled her ring finger.

Megan gasped and grabbed her hand, holding it up to the light. "Look at it sparkle!" She squared her gaze on Donovan. "You better take good care of her. She's my most favorite person in the whole world."

"She's mine as well."

"So, how did you do it?" Megan asked. "You were so cryptic in your message I have no idea what happened."

Alice linked her arm around her best friend's elbow. "I'm about to tell the committee. Come listen."

They finished the trek across the restaurant, and Alice explained everything that had happened. Christine's eyes widened, her lips parting as she listened with an expression of awe.

"The humans think a change in tides solved the issue," she said when Alice finished the story.

"Probably best if we let them," Alice said.

Christine shook Donovan's hand. "We owe you our thanks, Mr. Drake."

He slid his arm behind Alice's back, tugging her to his side. "Alice deserves all the credit. I was merely the conduit for her sacrifice."

She grinned. "You did promise the spirit of the creek you'd live here for the rest of your life."

He kissed her cheek. "That's not a sacrifice at all."

"Oh, Alice," Christine said, "I almost forgot to tell you. A city council member just resigned. His wife got a job in Dallas, so there's an open seat. I hope you'll consider running. We could use more supes in office."

"Maybe I will."

Donovan tugged his phone from his pocket, his brow furrowing as he looked at the screen. "Excuse me, I need to take this."

"Alice Drake has a nice ring to it." Megan offered her a chardonnay and clinked her glass to hers.

"It does, doesn't it?"

"I guess you'll be moving into Rainecourt Manor?"

"*Drake* Manor, and yes. If that's okay with Marty." She winked at the mongoose, who sat on the bar next to her, nibbling a slice of garlic bread.

Marty winked back, and though she didn't hear the wind breaking over the chatter in the room, the scent of pepperoni mixed with broccoli and eggs was unmistakable. They would have to work on his diet if her olfactory sense was to survive living with the gassy little guy.

Donovan approached, a look of uneasiness drawing his mouth into a frown. He stopped abruptly and looked at his familiar. "Seriously, Martin. People are trying to eat."

Marty only chittered in return, since there were mundies in the room.

"Who called?" Alice slipped her hand into Donovan's.

"That was my brother." His voice sounded wary.

"Which one?" Megan's eyes lit up.

"Griffin. I told him the matter had been dealt with, but he insists on paying a visit."

"That's nice of him." Alice patted his hand. "You two got along growing up, right? It was Matthias who was the butthead."

"When my father wasn't around, we did, but..." He shook his head.

"Well, your father's not around now. I'd like to meet your family."

He tucked a strand of hair behind her ear. "It appears you'll get your wish."

If Megan smiled any bigger, her face would have torn in two. "Griffin is coming here? You're sure?"

Donovan nodded. "Indeed."

Megan tossed her hair behind her shoulder. "Oh, goody."

PARANORMAL CHICK LIT

**The best paranormal chick lit books
on the virtual shelves!**

Who are we? We're a group of cray-cray authors who
thought it'd be totes fabu to all write and release
#paranormalchicklit books together. From witches to fae
to super sexy shifters, we've got the best #pcl in any flavor
you desire.

Visit Us on the Web
paranormalchicklit.com

ACKNOWLEDGMENTS

Special thanks to **Rebekka McCullough** for naming Alice and Megan's art gallery **Shifted Treasures**. It's the perfect name for their shop!

ALSO BY CARRIE PULKINEN

New Orleans Nocturnes Series

License to Bite

Shift Happens

Life's a Witch

Santa Got Run Over by a Vampire

Finders Reapers

Crescent City Wolf Pack Series

Werewolves Only

Beneath a Blue Moon

Bound by Blood

A Deal with Death

A Song to Remember

Crescent City Ghost Tours Series

Love and Ghosts

Love and Omens

ALSO BY CARRIE PULKINEN

Spirit Chasers Series

To Catch a Spirit

To Stop a Shadow

To Free a Phantom

Stand Alone Books

The Rest of Forever

Bewitching the Vampire

Soul Catchers

ABOUT THE AUTHOR

Carrie Pulkinen is a paranormal romance author who has always been fascinated with things that go bump in the night. Of course, when you grow up next door to a cemetery, the dead (and the undead) are hard to ignore. Pair that with her passion for writing and her love of a good happily-ever-after, and becoming a paranormal romance author seems like the only logical career choice.

Before she decided to turn her love of the written word into a career, Carrie spent the first part of her professional life as a high school journalism and yearbook teacher. She loves good chocolate and bad puns, and in her free time, she likes to read, drink wine, and travel with her family.

Connect with Carrie online:
www.CarriePulkinen.com

Made in the USA
Las Vegas, NV
02 February 2022

42887728R00121